PORNOGRAFIA

PORNOGRAFIA

by Witold Gombrowicz

Translated from the French
by Alastair Hamilton

Grove Press, Inc. New York

Library of Congress Catalog Card Number: 66–29765

First Evergreen Edition, 1968
First Printing

MANUFACTURED IN THE UNITED STATES OF AMERICA
BY THE BOOK PRESS INCORPORATED

Preface

A Polish author once wrote to me asking about the philosophical meaning of *Pornografia*.

I replied:

"Let us try to express ourselves as simply as possible. Man, as we know, aims at the absolute. At fulfillment. At truth, at God, at total maturity. . . To seize everything, to realize himself entirely—this is his imperative.

"Now, in *Pornografia* it seems to me that another of man's aims appears, a more secret one, undoubtedly, one which is in some way illegal: his need for the unfinished. . . for imperfection. . . for inferiority. . . for youth. . .

"One of the clearest scenes in this sense is the one in church, where the celebration of the Mass collapses under the force of Frederick's strained conscience, and with it God the Absolute, while, from the dark and cosmic void, comes a new, earthly, sensual idol composed of two minor beings who form a closed circle—because they are submitted to a mutual attraction.

"Another important scene is the assembly before Siemian's murder, when the adults feel incapable of killing him because they are aware of the weight of murder. The murder must therefore be committed by adolescents shifted onto a level of frivolity and irresponsibility—this is the only way it can be done.

"I have already mentioned this elsewhere, if only in my *Diary*, in a passage about the Retiro in Buenos Aires (1955): 'Youth seemed to me the highest value of life. . . but this "value" has a particularity undoubtedly invented by the devil himself: being youth it is below the level of all values.'

"These last words ('below all values') explained why I have been unable to take root in any contemporary existentialism. Existentialism tries to re-establish value, while for me the 'undervalue,' the 'insufficiency,' the 'underdevelopment' are closer to man than any value. I believe the formula 'Man wants to be God' expresses very well the nostalgia of existentialism, while I set up another immeasurable formula against it: 'Man wants to be young.'

"In my opinion the ages of man serve as a tool for this dialectic between the fulfilled and the unfulfilled, between the value and the undervalue. This is why I give such an enormously dramatic part to youth. And this is why my universe is degraded, as though someone had taken the spirit by the scruff of the neck and immersed it in frivolity and inferiority.

"But remember that for me philosophy has no meaning; it is none of my business. My sole intention is to exploit certain possibilities of a theme. I search for the 'beauties' peculiar to this conflict. . . "

* * *

Is this clear? It is said that a work explains itself, that the author's commentaries are superfluous. On the whole that is true! But contemporary art is not always easily accessible and it is sometimes useful for the author to take the reader by the hand and show him the way.

* * *

Maybe I should say who I am and where I come from.

I am the author of the following works in Polish: *Bakakai* (short stories); *Yvonne, Princess of Burgundy* (comedy); *Ferdydurke* (novel); *The Marriage* (drama); *The Trans-Atlantic* (novel); *Pornografia* (novel). And finally, my *Diary* from 1953 to 1961.

I was almost unknown until 1957. An immigrant in the Argentine.

In 1957 the Polish government, in a moment of fleeting liberalism, allowed my books to be reprinted. The enormous and unexpected success of this enterprise was such that I was banned once more and it became illegal to write about me. (Such is the musical chairs that we writers of certain countries play with our people, even those who, like me, do not meddle in politics.)

* * *

Ferdydurke is undoubtedly my basic work, the best introduction to what I am and what I represent. Written twenty years later, *Pornografia* originates from *Ferdydurke*. I should therefore say a few words about this book.

It is the grotesque story of a gentleman who becomes a child because other people treat him like one. *Ferdydurke* is intended to reveal the Great Immaturity of humanity. Man, as he is described in this book, is an opaque and neutral being who has to express himself by certain means of behavior and therefore becomes, from outside—for others—far more definite and precise than he is for himself. Hence a tragic disproportion between his secret immaturity and the mask he assumes when he deals with other people. All he can do is to adapt himself internally to his mask, as though he really were what he appears to be.

It can therefore be said that the man of *Ferdydurke* is created by others, that men create each other by imposing forms on each other, or what we would call *façons d'être*.

Ferdydurke was published in 1937 before Sartre formulated his theory of the *regard d'autrui*. But it is owing to the popularization of Sartrean concepts that this aspect of my book has been better understood and assimilated.

And yet *Ferdydurke* ventures on other, lesser known ground, the word "form" is associated with the word "immaturity." How can this Ferdydurkean man be described? Created by form he is created from outside, in other words unauthentic and deformed. To be a man means never to be oneself.

He is also a constant producer of form: he secretes form tirelessly, just as the bee secretes honey.

But he is also at odds with his own form. *Ferdydurke* is the description of the struggle of man with his own expression, of the torture of humanity on the Procrustean bed of form.

Immaturity is not always innate or imposed by others. There is also an immaturity which culture batters us against when it submerges us and we do not manage to hoist ourselves up to its level. We are "infantilized" by all "higher" forms. Man, tortured by his mask, fabricates secretly, for his own usage, a sort of "subculture": a world made out of the refuse of a higher world of culture, a domain of trash, immature myths, inadmissible passions. . . a secondary domain of compensation. That is where a certain shameful poetry is born, a certain compromising beauty. . . .

Are we not close to *Pornografia?*

* * *

Yes, *Pornografia* springs from *Ferdydurke*: it is a particularly irritating case of the Ferdydurkean world: the Younger creating the Older. When the Older creates the Younger everything works very well from a social and cultural point of view. But if the Older is submitted to the Younger—what darkness! What perversity and shame! How many traps! And yet Youth, biologically superior, physically more beautiful, has no trouble in charming and conquering the adult, already poisoned by death. From this point of view *Pornografia* is bolder than *Ferdydurke* which uses, above all, sarcasm and irony—and humor implicates distance. In those days I tackled my themes from above and it could be claimed that in *Ferdydurke* I am struggling proudly against immaturity. And yet you can already perceive an ambiguous note which could imply that this opponent of immaturity is mortally in love with immaturity.

In *Pornografia* I have given up the distance lent by humor. It is not a satire but a noble, a classical novel. . . The novel of two middle-aged men and a couple of adolescents; a sensually metaphysical novel. What a disgrace!

* * *

I quote again from my *Diary*:

"One of my aesthetic and spiritual aims is to discover a more open, more dramatic access to Youth. To reveal its ties with maturity so that they should complete each other."

And:

"I do not believe in a nonerotic philosophy. I do not trust any desexualized idea.

"It is hard to believe that Hegel's *Science of Logic* or Kant's *Critique of Pure Reason* could have been conceived if their authors had not kept a certain distance from their bodies. But pure conscience, when it is hardly realized, must be steeped again in the body, in sex, in Eros; the artist must plunge the philosopher in enchantment, charm, and grace."

One more comment, although I might be suspected of megalomania: "And what if *Pornografia* were an attempt to

renew Polish eroticism? . . . An attempt to revive an eroticism which would bear a stronger relationship to our destiny
and our recent history—composed of rape, slavery, and
boyish squabbles—a descent to the dark limits of the conscience and the body?"

* * *

I am more and more inclined to present what seem to
me the most complex themes in a simple, naive form.
Pornografia is written in the style of a Polish "provincial
novel"; it is as though I were going for a ride in a charabanc,
rendered obsolete by the poison of the *dernier cri* (an old
fashioned cry, of pain, of course). Am I right in thinking
that the more literature is bold and inaccessible the more
it should return to old and easy forms, familiar to the
reader?

K. A. Jelenski, to whom my work owes so many and such
precious suggestions, considered that *Pornografia* presented
itself too definitely; he advised me to cover some of my
traces, like animals and certain painters. But I am already
tired of all the misunderstandings which have accumulated
between me and my reader and if I could I would have
limited his liberty to interpret me still more.

—W. G.

PART ONE

1

I shall tell you about another experience I had, undoubtedly the most fatal of all.

In those days, in 1943, I was staying in former Poland, in former Warsaw, at the depths of the *fait accompli*. In silence. The dilapidated group of my old friends and companions from the former cafés, the Zodiak, the Ziemianska, the Ips, met every Tuesday in a small flat in Krucza Street where we drank and tried to go on living like artists, writers, and thinkers. . . renewing our old conversations, our past discussions about art. . . I can still see them, sitting or lounging on the sofas in the smoky rooms, one or two of them a trifle cadaverous and worn, but all shouting and shrieking. One shouted: "God"; another: "art"; a third: "the people"; a fourth: "the proletariat." We talked ourselves hoarse, and it went on and on—God, art, the people, the proletariat. But one day a middle-aged man appeared, dark and thin, with a hooked nose. He formally introduced himself to everybody, and then hardly spoke a word.

He ceremoniously thanked his host for the glass of vodka he was offered, and equally ceremoniously said: "May I bother you for a match?" . . . He then waited for the match, and waited. . . and when he had been given it, set about lighting his cigarette. In the meantime the discussion raged on—God, art, the people, the proletariat—and the stench

13

began to pervade the air. Someone asked: "What good wind brings you, Frederick?" To which he replied, most explicitly: "Eva told me that Pientak often comes here, so I looked in because I've got four rabbit skins and a leather sole to sell." And, to prove it, he showed us his four rabbit skins wrapped up in a piece of paper.

He was offered some tea, which he drank; a lump of sugar remained on his saucer—he stretched out his hand toward it, but obviously considered his gesture pointless, and withdrew his hand. Since this gesture was even more pointless, however, he stretched out his hand once more, took the lump of sugar, and ate it—not for pleasure but to behave consistently. . . toward the sugar or toward us?. . . Clearly wanting to eradicate this unfavorable impression, he coughed, then, so as the cough should not seem pointless, pulled out his pocket handkerchief—but did not dare blow his nose and simply moved his foot. Moving his foot doubtlessly entailed other complications, so he decided to sit silent and motionless. This strange behavior (because in fact all he ever did was "to behave," he "behaved" the whole time) aroused my curiosity at the first encounter, and, in the course of the following months, I came closer to this man who proved to be by no means uncultured and also had a certain artistic experience (he had once worked in the theater). In short, we collaborated in small deals which earned us a meager living. But that did not last long, because one day I received a letter from Hippo, my friend Hippolytus S., a landowner from the Sandomierz district, inviting us to stay—Hippolytus added that he thought we might be of some assistance in his business affairs in Warsaw and wanted to discuss them with us. "It's quite peaceful down here, of course, except for the occasional raid by one of the gangs—you see, there is hardly any discipline. . . If you both come it will be more enjoyable."

Should we go? Both of us? I had fearful doubts about the journey. . . What, take him so that he could continue his game down there, in the country?. . . And his body which was so. . . so specific?. . . Travel with him regardless of his "obvious but hidden indecency?" . . . Look after somebody so "compromised" and therefore so "compromising?". . . Expose myself to this continual "dialogue" with. . . with whom? And his knowledge, his knowledge of. . . ? And his cunning, his ruses? Yes, it did not seem very enticing, and yet his eternal game made him so different, so alien to our common drama, so detached from our interminable discussions—God, the people, the proletariat, art—that it seemed refreshing, a relief. . . And in spite of it all he was so immaculate, prudent and level-headed! Oh well, come on then! It *is* so much more enjoyable if we both go! At last we squeezed into the crowded railway carriage, and the train slowly creaked out of the station.

Three o'clock in the afternoon. It was misty. Frederick, standing hunched under the weight of an old woman, a child's foot sticking into his chin, was as formal and well behaved as ever. Neither of us spoke. The train jolted us and hurled us against each other, into a congealed mass. . . through the window I could just see the sleepy, blue fields as we hurtled past. . . it was the same vast plain I had seen hundreds of times, the misty skyline, the checkered earth, trees whizzing by, a house, the figure of a woman. . . always the same, expected thing. . . And yet not the same thing, precisely because it is the same thing! Unexpected, unknown, incomprehensible, almost inconceivable! The child started howling, the old woman sneezed. . .

This bitter smell. . . The eternal sadness of a train journey, this sadness learned by heart, the ascending and descending line of the telegraph wires or the embankment, the sudden appearance of a tree in the window, of a telegraph pole, a signalman's hut, the landscape sliding swiftly past, its incessant retreat. . . as a chimney or a hill on the horizon rush into view. . . before vanishing into nothingness in a slow curve. Frederick was in front of me; his head, separated from me by two or three heads, was very close— he sat in silence, absorbed by the journey. . . and the presence of other bodies, importunate, invasive, and insolent, made my silent tête-à-tête with him so agonizing, so profound that. . . I would rather not have traveled with him and wished our plans had fallen through! For, in a corporal context, he was no more than a body among other bodies. . . but at the same time he existed—on his own, inexorably. . . There was nothing to be done. One could neither elude him, nor neglect him, nor efface him, he was in this crowd of people and existed. . . And his journey, his leap into space, were not comparable to anyone else's—it was a far more important, almost dangerous journey.

From time to time he smiled at me, said something obviously intended to make his presence bearable, less oppressive. I suddenly realized how hazardous it was to remove him from the town, to let him loose in the plains, in the wide-open spaces where his singular inner qualities could come into their own. He too must have realized this because I never saw him so silent, so insignificant. At one point the twilight, that substance which engulfs all forms, began to erase him and he faded away in the jolting, hurtling railway carriage, as it tore into the night, inducing a state of nonexistence. But that did not attenuate his presence, which merely dissolved behind a veil of invisibility. . . he existed just the same. Suddenly the light went on, thrusting him into view, revealing his chin, the lines at the corners of his mouth, his ears. . . but he did not budge and stood staring at the swaying telegraph wire—he was there! The train drew to another halt—from somewhere behind me came shouts and the sound of boots, the crowd lurched into us—something was happening, but he remained there! The train moved off again. It was dark outside, and the engine spat sparks as the carriage entered the night.—Why had I brought him with me? Why had I condemned myself to this presence which, instead of resting me, exhausted me? The journey lasted for countless sleepy hours, interspersed with halts and police investigations, gradually becoming an end in itself, somnolent and obstinate, until we got to Cmielow and found ourselves with our luggage on a path by the side of the railway line. The bright quiver of the train in the abating roar. The silence, a strange breeze and the stars. A cricket.

Myself, suddenly removed from the bustle of a long journey, on this path, next to Frederick standing, his coat over his arm, in silence. Where were we? What was it? And yet I knew this district, the breeze was familiar—but where were we? Over there, at an angle, stood the familiar building of the Cmielow railway station and a couple of lamps swaying in the dark, but. . . where, on which planet had we disembarked? Frederick stood next to me—he just stood. And then we walked to the station, myself in front, him behind. There were the break, the horses and the driver—the break was familiar and familiar, too, was the way the driver raised his cap—so why did I observe them so closely?

I got into the break, followed by Frederick, and we drove off. The sandy path in the light of the black sky, on either side the black shapes of trees or bushes, we went through the village of Brzustowa, the shimmer of whitewashed planks, and the bark of a dog—what a strange bark!—in front of me the driver's back—what a strange back!—and next to me my silent, polite companion. The invisible ground rocked and jolted the break, the pits of darkness and the thick shadows between the trees blocked our view. To hear the sound of my own voice I asked the driver:

"How is it around here? Quiet?"

And I heard him reply:

"It is right now. There are some gangs in the woods. But lately it's been pretty quiet."

The face was invisible and the voice was the same—therefore it was not the same. In front of me nothing but his back, and, for a moment, I wanted to bend forward and have a good look at this back, but I stopped myself. . . because Frederick. . . was there, next to me. And he was curiously silent. With him next to me I preferred not to have a good look at anybody. . . because I suddenly realized that the being sitting next to me was radical in his silence, radical to the point of insanity. Yes, he was an extremist, an extremist to the last degree. No, his was no ordinary existence, it was something infinitely aggressive, exerted to an extent I would never, until that day, have believed possible. I preferred not to have a good look at anybody—not even the driver whose back was crushing us like a mountain, as the invisible ground rocked and jolted the break and the surrounding twilight, pierced by a few shiny stars, blocked our view. The rest of the journey continued in silence. At last we entered a long drive, the horses quickened their pace —the gate, the watchman, the dogs, the heavy creaking of the bolts—Hippo holding a lamp. . .

"Thank God, you're here at last!"

Was it really he? I was struck and, at the same time, repelled by his bloated, red cheeks, bursting out. . . he looked as though he were bloated by a tumor that had distorted his limbs and stretched his flesh in every direction so that his repulsively flourishing body was like an erupting volcano of meat. . . and in his riding boots he flaunted his apocalyptic paws, while his eyes peeped out between lumps of fat. But he drew me to him and embraced me. He whispered shyly:

"I've grown bloated, damn it. I've put on weight. Why? Everything, I suppose."

And looking at his pudgy fingers he repeated with infinite bitterness, softly, to himself:

"I've put on weight. Why? Everything, I suppose."

And he thundered:

"This is my wife!"

And murmured, to himself:

"This is my wife."

And he shouted:

"And this is my darling Henia, my sweet little Henia!"

And whispered to himself, almost inaudibly:

"And this is my darling Henia, my sweet little Henia."

Then, hospitable and flourishing, he turned to us:

"How good of you to come, but please, Witold, introduce your friend. . ." He closed his eyes and repeated. . . his lips went on moving. Frederick gallantly, ceremoniously, kissed his hostess' hand, and a distant smile shone through her melancholy, and her svelte figure trembled. . . We plunged into the turmoil of introductions, our hosts showed us into the house, we sat down, they paid us the customary compliments, we returned them—after that interminable journey—while the paraffin lamp gave out its dreamy light. Dinner was served by a lackey. Our eyes were heavy with sleep. Vodka. Struggling with our exhaustion we strove to hear and to understand what was being said. The conversation was about every sort of difficulty—with the A.K.,* or the Germans, the gangs, the administration, the Polish police, requisitions—about constant fear and violence, evident from the additional iron bars on the shutters, the heavy bolts on the doors, the weapons glinting in the

---

* A.K.—*Armia Krajowa*, the Polish resistance movement.—*Tr. note.*

corner. . . "The Siemiechow's property was burnt down, in Rudniki the overseer's legs were broken, I had the house full of refugees from Poznan. . . the worst of it all is one can't tell what's going to happen next. At Ostrowiec, at Bodzechow, where the factory workers live, they're just waiting for a chance. . . at the moment it's pretty quiet, but if the Front comes any nearer it's going to blow up! It's going to blow up! Then you'll see the slaughter and the fireworks! Then you'll see the fireworks!" he yelled, then whispered to himself, thoughtfully:

"Then you'll see the fireworks."

And he shouted:

"The worst of it is there's nowhere to go!"

And he whispered:

"The worst of it is there's nowhere to go."

The lamp. An interminable dinner. Drowsiness. Hippo's vast figure smeared with the thick sauce of sleep, his wife dissolving into the distance, Frederick, the moths bumping into the lamp, moths in the lamp, moths around the lamp, the steep and narrow staircase, the candle. I collapsed onto a bed and fell asleep. The next morning, a triangle of sun on the wall. A voice below the window. I got up and opened the shutters. The early morning.

2

Clumps of trees between the graceful curves of the paths, the garden sloped gently down to the lime trees behind which could be perceived the hidden surface of a pond—oh! all that green glistening with the dew! And when we went out into the courtyard after breakfast—the house, white, with two floors and its mansard roof, surrounded by firs and thuyas, flower beds and paths, which astonished us like a vision from the past, from the distant days before the war. . . and in its very permanence it seemed more real than the war. . . but at the same time the feeling that it was not true, that it was at odds with reality, transformed it into a theatrical décor. . . finally, the house, the park, the sky, and the fields became both theatrical and real. But here came our host, in all his enormity, a green jacket on his bloated body, and he approached us just as he used to, waving to us from the distance and asking if we had slept well. Chatting idly we went through the gateway into the fields and gazed over the sweep of country, undulating in the wind, and Hippo spoke to Frederick about the harvest and the profits, occasionally crushing little clods of earth with his foot. We came back toward the house. Hippo's wife appeared on the balcony and shouted good morning to us as a little boy ran across the lawn, the son of the cook, perhaps? So we ambled through the morning—the repetition of other mornings—but it was not so simple—because the landscape suddenly seemed somehow withered and again it struck me that everything, although it remained the same, was different. What an absurd idea, what an oppressively disguised thought! Frederick was walking along beside me, illuminated by the bright daylight in such a way that one could perceive the hairs sticking out of his ears and all the pores of his pale, wizened skin, Frederick, I repeat, bent, enfeebled and round-shouldered, in pince-nez, his nervous mouth twitching, his hands in his pockets—the typical city intellectual in the country. . . And yet, in this contrast, the countryside was no longer victorious, the trees lost their assurance, the sky seemed altered, the cow no longer offered the anticipated resistance, the eternity of the countryside now seemed ruffled, uncertain, troubled. . . And Frederick, yes, Frederick now seemed more real than the grass. More real? An exhausting, disquieting, foul idea, even somewhat hysterical, even provocative, invasive, destructive. . . and I did not know whether it was Frederick who had given me this idea, or the war, the revolution, the occupation. . . or both? And yet he behaved impeccably, questioned Hippolytus about the farming, saying the things he was expected to say—and suddenly we saw Henia coming across the lawn. The sun burnt our skin. Our eyes were dry and our lips chapped. She said:

"Mama is ready. I've had the horses harnessed."

"To go to church, to Mass, it's Sunday," explained Hippolytus. And he added softly to himself:

"To go to church, to Mass."

And loudly:

"If you want to join us we'll be delighted, but you're not obliged to. I believe in tolerance, don't I? I'm going, and as long as I'm here I'll go! As long as there's a church I'll go to church! With my wife and daughter, what's more, *and* in a carriage—I don't need to hide—Let people see me—Let them stare to their hearts' content, let them photograph me!"

And he murmured:

"Let them photograph me!"

But Frederick was already stressing our eagerness to go to Mass. We drove along in the carriage, its wheels creaking as they sank into the sandy ruts—and when we reached the top of the hill we saw the vast expanse of low fields, low under the curiously high sky, cowering in an immobilized surge. There, in the distance, was the railway track. I wanted to laugh. The carriage, the horses, the driver, the hot smell of sweat and varnish, the dust, the sun, a fly on my face, and the creak of the wheels on the sand—It was all centuries old and nothing, not one single thing, had changed! But on the hill we caught our breath in the cool waft of the space, of the space which ended in the shimmering skyline of the Mountains of the Holy Cross, and the perversity of this trip almost gave me a start, because it was as though we had stepped out of an oleograph—a dead photograph from an old family album—and the obsolete vehicle on the hill could be seen for miles, thereby making the country-side particularly ironical, cruelly disdainful. The perversity of our deceased journey spread to the bluish landscape, turning and changing imperceptibly as we gradually ad-vanced. Frederick, sitting on the back seat next to Maria, looked around in every direction and admired the color scheme as though he really were going to church. Never, do I think, have I seen him so sociable and polite! We drove around the curve down into the ravine where the village began, and the mud. . . .

I recall (and this is of a certain importance for the events which will subsequently be related) that my dominant feel-ing was one of vacuity and again, as on the previous night, I wanted to lean out and look the driver in the face. . . But that was impossible, it was not done. . . so we remained behind his impenetrable back and our journey continued behind his back. We drove into the village of Grocholice, to our left a stream and to our right scattered houses and fences, a hen and a goose, a trough and a pond, a man or a woman in their Sunday clothes hurrying toward the church. . . the sleepy serenity of a village on a Sunday. But it was as though our death, leaning over a pool, were presenting its own image, so perfectly was the obsolete antiquity of our entrance reflected in the immemorial existence of the village, and so loudly did it resound in this insanity—which was, moreover, only a mask used to hide something. . . But what? Any meaning, every meaning. . . of the war, the revolution, violence, incontinence, misery, starvation, despair, a curse or a blessing. . . every meaning, I repeat, would have been too feeble to pierce the crystal of this idyll, so that the image we provided, which had long been antiquated and lacking in substance, remained unchangeable. Frederick was conversing politely with Maria— but was it not simply to avoid saying something else that he sustained this banal conversation? We finally reached the low wall around the church and started getting out of the carriage—but I no longer knew what was what— whether the steps leading to the square were ordinary steps or whether. . . ? Frederick offered Maria his arm, after having taken off his hat, and ceremoniously led her to the church, before the eyes of the curious spectators—but maybe he only did it to avoid doing something else?—and behind them Hippo, who had managed to clamber out of the carriage and plunge his enormous frame forward, through the crowd, determined and impregnable, knowing that the next day they could slaughter him like a pig, advanced to spite the hatred, looking sinister and resigned.

The landlord! But maybe he was only being a landlord so as not to be something else?

But, as soon as we were engulfed in the twilight where lighted candles were stuck like nails, where a whining chant welled up from the coarse, prostrate throng. . . all the latent ambiguity vanished—as though an invisible hand, more powerful than ours, had re-established the sanctifying order of the Mass. Hippolytus, who had until that moment ardently and passionately acted the role of the landlord to save himself from being devoured, sat, suddenly serene and noble, in the family pew, and nodded to the family of the administrator of Ikania who sat opposite. The Mass had not yet begun, the priest had not yet appeared at the foot of the altar, the congregation was left to its humble, tender, strident, awkward chant, which kept it well under control and made it as harmless as a dog on a leash. What serenity, at last, what a relief: here, in this stone sanctuary, the peasant became the peasant, the master the master, the Mass the Mass, the stone stone and everything returned to itself.

And yet Frederick, who had taken his place next to Hippolytus, knelt down. . . and this troubled me a little for it seemed perhaps slightly exaggerated. . . and I could not help thinking that he had knelt down to avoid doing anything other than kneeling down. . . but the bell rang, the priest came in carrying the chalice and, after placing it on the altar, bowed down before it. The bell rang again. And suddenly I felt so moved, so deeply moved that I dropped to my knees and, in my wild emotion, I almost prayed. . . But Frederick! It seemed to me, and I suspected, that Frederick, on his knees, was "praying" too—I was even sure, yes, knowing his lack of integrity I was certain that he was not pretending but was really "praying" for the benefit of others and for his own benefit, but his prayer was no more than a screen to conceal the enormity of his "non-prayer". . . . it was an act of expulsion, of "eccentricity" which cast us out of this church into the infinite space of absolute disbelief, a negative act, the very act of negation. And what was going on? What was happening? I had never seen anything like it and I had never believed that that could happen. What exactly had happened? Strictly speaking: nothing, strictly speaking it was as though a hand had withdrawn the substance and content from the Mass—and the priest continued—and the priest continued to move, to kneel, to go from one end of the altar to the other, and the acolytes rang the bells and the smoke from the censers rose in spirals, but the whole content was evaporating like gas out of a balloon, and the Mass collapsed in its appalling impotence—limp and sagging—unable to procreate! And this loss of content was a murder committed out on a limb, outside ourselves, outside the Mass, by the mute but lethal commentary of a member of the congregation. And against that the Mass had no means of defense, because it had happened as the result of some subsidiary interpretation; nobody actually in the church could have resisted the Mass and even Frederick was participating as correctly as possible. . . and when he killed it it was only in effigy, one might almost say. But this commentary, this murderous criticism was an act of cruelty—the act of a sharp, cold, penetrating, pitiless consciousness. . . and I suddenly understood that it was insane to have brought this man into a church, for God's sake, that should have been avoided at all costs! For him church was the worst place in the world!

But it was too late! The process taking place before my eyes was revealing reality *in crudo*. . . it began by destroying salvation and in this way nothing could hope to save these repulsive peasant faces, stripped of any style and displayed raw, like scraps of meat on a butcher's stall. They were no longer the "people," they were no longer "peasants," or even "men," they were simple creatures, for what they were worth, and their natural filth was suddenly cut off from grace. But the wild anarchy of this multiheaded, tawny crowd corresponded to the no less arrogant shamelessness of our own faces which ceased being "intelligent" or "cultivated" or "delicate," and became like caricatures without a model, caricatures which had ceased representing anything and which were as bare as behinds! And these two explosions of monstrosity, the lordly and the boorish, blended in the gesture of the priest who was celebrating. . . what? What? Nothing. . . And yet that is not all.

The church was no longer a church. Space had broken in, but it was a cosmic, black space and it was no longer happening on earth, or rather the earth was turning into a planet suspended in the void of the universe, the cosmos was present, we were in the center of it. To a point when the flickering flame of the candles and even the daylight which filtered through the stained-glass windows turned as black as ink. We were no longer in church, nor in this village, nor on earth, but, in accordance with reality—somewhere suspended in the cosmos with our candles and light and it was there, in infinity, that we were playing our curious games with each other, like monkeys grimacing into space. It was a very special game, there, somewhere in the galaxy, a human challenge in darkness, the execution of curious movements and strange grimaces in space. And yet this drowning in space was accompanied by an extraordinary rise of the concrete, we were in the cosmos, but as though we were in something terrifyingly definite, determined in every detail. The bells rang for the elevation. Frederick knelt.

This time, by kneeling down, he dispatched the Mass as one rings the neck of a chicken and the Mass went on, by now mortally wounded and staggering like a drunkard. *Ite, missa est.* And, ah, what a triumph! What a victory over the Mass! What pride! As though this liquidation represented a long-awaited end: alone, at last, all alone, with nobody and nothing except myself, alone in complete darkness. . . I had reached my limit, I had reached darkness. Bitter the end, bitter the taste of victory, and bitter the goal! But it was proud and dizzy, branded by the pitiless immaturity of the at last autonomous mind. It was terrifying, too, and, with no support, I felt in myself as in the hands of a monster, capable of doing everything, of doing anything, anything with me! The aridity of pride. The icy finality. Severity and void. And then? And then? The Mass was ending, I looked around sleepily, I was tired, oh, we had to go out, go back home, to Pogorna, along that sandy path. . . but at a certain moment my gaze. . . my eyes. . . panic-stricken and heavy. . . Yes, something attracted them. . . my eyes. . . Oppressive and seductive. . . Yes. What? What attracted me? What tempted me? The miraculous, like certain veiled spots in our dreams, made more desirable by their inaccessibility and around which we circle with a mute cry, in the confusion of an agonizing longing.

I circled around it thus, still fearful and uncertain. . . but already deliciously abandoned to the sweet violence which seized me—charmed me—enticed me—enchanted me—tempted and subdued me. . . And the contrast between the cosmic ice of this night and this spring bubbling with delight was such that I caught myself thinking vaguely that it was God and a miracle, God and a miracle. . .

But what was it?

It was. . . a fragment of cheek and a piece of neck. . . belonging to someone in the congregation a few steps away from us. . .

Oh, it was unbelievable! It was. . .

(a boy)

(a boy)

And, having understood it was only (a boy) I began to recover from my ecstasy. In fact I had hardly seen him! I had just seen a bit of ordinary skin—on the cheek and the neck. Now he suddenly moved and this meaningless movement cut right through me. What an unlikely attraction!

But it was (a boy).

No more than (a boy).

How awkward! A sixteen-year-old neck, close-cropped hair and the ordinary skin of (the boy) with a few little chaps and a (youthful) bearing—perfectly ordinary—so why was I trembling? Ah. . . now I could see the contour of the nose because he had tilted his head slightly to the left—still perfectly ordinary, and, at an angle, I could see the ordinary face of (the boy)—but perfectly ordinary! He was not a peasant. A student? A probationer? Nothing special about this (youthful) face, untroubled, slightly defiant, a face that would chew the ends of pencils, play football or billiards, and the collar of his jacket concealed his shirt collar, his neck was sunburned. And yet my heart was beating very fast. And he emitted an aura of divinity, marvelously captivating and enchanting in the infinite void of this night, a source of heat and living light. Charm. In vain I wondered why. Why had his insignificance suddenly become so significant?

Frederick? Did he know it, had he seen it, had he noticed it too?. . . But suddenly the congregation moved, the Mass was ended, they were slowly pushing toward the door. And I was among them. Henia was in front of me, her back and her scholarly little neck, and this came before me and, once there, impressed itself so deeply—and blended so harmoniously, so perfectly with that other neck. . . and suddenly I realized, it was easy and entailed no effort, yes: this

neck and the other neck. These two necks. These necks
were. . .

What? What was it? It was as though her (girl's) neck
broke away to join that other (boy's) neck, this neck
dragged by the neck and dragging the other neck by the
neck! Please excuse the clumsiness of these metaphors. It
is not so easy for me to discuss them (and one day I shall
have to explain why I put the words *boy* and *girl* in parentheses, yes, this too remains to be explained). Her movements, as they preceded me in the hot, hurrying crowd,
seemed to "concern him," in a certain way, and were like
the passionate, languid complement of his movements in
the same crowd, close by. Really? Was I wrong? Suddenly
I saw her hand hanging by her body, crushed into her flesh
by the pressure of the crowd, and this crushed hand abandoned her flesh to him in the intimacy and the throng of
all these crowded bodies. It is true, all of her was "for him."
And he, further on, walking peacefully with the congregation, was straining toward her, for her. This love, this wild
desire advanced so calmly with the crowd in affected indifference! Ah, that was it!—I now knew what secret had
attracted me to him at the first moment.

We emerged from the church into the sunny square, and
the people dispersed—but they—he and she—appeared to
me in full. She, wearing a light blouse, a navy blue skirt, a
white collar, standing aside, waiting for her parents, was
fastening the clasp on her prayer book. He. . . went a few
paces toward the wall around the church, and, standing on
tiptoe, looked over the other side—I do not know why. Did
they know each other? Although they were each on their
own, their passionate suitability seemed all the more obvious: they were made for each other. I blinked—the little
square was white, green, blue, hot—I blinked. He for her,
and she for him, far away from each other, not showing any

interest in each other, and the impression was so strong that the (boy's) lips not only seemed made for her lips but for her whole body—and her body seemed supported by his legs!

And yet I think I went too far in this last sentence. . . Would it not have been better to say simply that they were exceptionally well suited to each other. . . and not only sexually? It sometimes happens that we see a couple and say: "They're very well suited," but in this case their suitability, I can call it that, seemed all the more responsive because of its immaturity. . . I really do not know if I am making myself clear. . . and yet this adolescent sensuality had an unusual gleam, like a supernatural treasure, because they represented supreme happiness for each other, th most precious and the most important possession. An there, on that square, under that sun, dazed and baffled, could not understand why they did not display a grea interest in each other, did not fly toward each other! S stood on her own and he stood on his own!

Sunday, the country, the heat, a sleepy indolence, the church, nobody in a hurry to go home, little groups assembled. Maria touched her face with her finger tip, as though she were examining the texture of the skin, Hippolytus discussed quotas with the administrator of Ikania, next to them, Frederick, courteous, his hands in his jacket pockets, a guest. . . ah, this image deleted the black chasm in which this agonizingly bright flame had just appeared. . . only one thought upset me: had Frederick noticed it? Did he know?

Frederick?

Hippolytus asked the administrator:

"What about the potatoes?"

"Well, we can always deliver half a hundredweight."

The (boy) came up to us.

"This is my son Karol," said the administrator, pushing him toward Frederick, who shook his hand. He greeted everybody, one after the other. Henia said to her mother:

"Look! Mrs. Galecka's better!"

"Well, shall we call on the priest?" asked Hippolytus, and immediately murmured: "What's the use?" and thundered: "Come on, gentlemen, it's time to go back!"

We shook the administrator's hand and got into the carriage together with Karol (well, what does that mean?) who sat next to the driver. We started off, the axles of the rubber wheels creaking in the ruts; the sandy path in the quivering and soporific air, a gilded fly buzzing—and, from the top of the hill, the uneven patches of the fields and the railway track in the distance, there where the forest began. We drove on. Frederick, sitting next to Henia, spoke at length about the golden blue sheen in the air, so typical of the region and due, he explained, to the minute particles of loess. We drove on.

3

The carriage jolted. Karol was sitting next to the driver, on the driver's seat. She was on the front seat and where her head ended he began, as though he were perched on a floor above her, turning his back to us, only visible as a faceless silhouette—his shirt puffed out with the wind—and the combination of her face and his lack of face, her seeing face complementing his blind spine, filled me with a feeling of warm, obscure duplication. . . They were not particularly handsome, neither he nor she—no more than is normal at that age—but they were beauty itself in their magic circle, in their mutual desire and enchantment—something in which nobody had any right to participate. They were for themselves—strictly between themselves. Especially since they were so (young). So I had no right to stare at them and I tried not to see them, but since Frederick was sitting in front of me, next to Henia on the front seat, I again stubbornly wondered: had he seen them? Did he know? And I watched his every glance, glances which feigned indifference but which sneaked across surreptitiously and greedily.

And the others? What did the others know? It was hard to believe that something which seemed so obvious could have escaped (the girl's) parents—so, that afternoon, on my way to the cowshed with Hippolytus, I tried to steer the conversation onto Karol. But it was hard for me to ask straight questions about (the boy) who, what a disgrace! had so excited me, and, as for Hippo, the subject cannot have seemed worth a thought. "Karol, oh yes, a good boy, the administrator's son; he was with the partisans and he was sent near Lublin where he did something silly. . . oh, nothing important, he pinched something, wounded somebody, one of his comrades or his leader, I don't know, anyhow nothing important; but he had to beat it and he came home.—Since he's got it in for his father, the rascal, and they're always going for each other, I'm having him to stay for a bit—He's a good mechanic and there's no harm in having a few more people in the house in case. . . —In case. . ." he repeated as though he were reveling in it and crushed a clod of earth with his foot. And he suddenly changed the subject. Did this sixteen-year-old's biography not seem worth the telling? Or maybe he thought it preferable to play down (the boy's) pranks so as not to make them seem too important? Had he wounded or killed his comrade? I wondered. But even if he had killed that could be excused by his age, which obliterated everything. I asked if he and Henia had known each other long.

"Since they were children," he replied, tapping a cow lightly on the rump, and he added: "She's Dutch! A good milker! Sick, damn it!" That was all I could discover. So neither he nor his wife had noticed anything—anything at all serious, at least, which could have aroused their vigilance. . . How was that possible? I told myself that if the affair had been more adult—slightly less immature—slightly less boyish-and-girlish. . . but it was drowned in the insufficiency of their age.

Frederick? What had he noticed? After the church, after having slaughtered, having throttled the Mass, I simply had to know if he knew—and the idea of his not knowing would

have been almost unbearable to me! The worst thing was
that I could not in any way connect these two distinct states
of mind—the first, the black one, conceived by Frederick,
and the other fresh and passionate one caused by Karol and
Henia—these two states of mind continued to exist in me,
separate and heterogeneous. But how could Frederick be
expected to discover anything if there was nothing between
them. . . ? and for me it was fantastic, almost inconceivable,
that they could both behave as though they were not seduc-
ing each other! I waited for them in vain to betray themselves. Their indifference seemed incredible! I watched
Karol at lunch. A child, but a corrupt child. An attractive
murderer. A smiling slave. A young soldier. A tough soft-
ness. A cruel, gory game. But this laughing, or rather, smiling child, had been "taken in hand" by men—he had the
silent gravity of an adolescent who had participated at an
early age in adult matters, pushed into the war, brought up
by the army—and when he buttered his bread, when he ate,
he displayed the temperance acquired from hunger. Occasionally his voice became gloomy and dull. He was something like iron. Like a leather thong, a freshly felled tree.
At first glance he was perfectly ordinary, serene and friendly,
obedient and even eager. Torn between the child and the
grown man (and this made him both innocently naive and
pitilessly experienced) he was neither the one nor the
other, but he was a third term, he was youth, violent and
uncontrolled, surrendering him to cruelty, restraint and
obedience, and condemning him to slavery and humiliation.
He was inferior because he was young. Imperfect because
he was young. Sensual because he was young. Carnal because he was young. Destructive because he was young. And,
in his very youthfulness, he was despicable. The oddest
thing of all was that his smile, the most elegant thing about
him, was the very mechanism that dragged him into humili-

ation, because this child could not defend himself, disarmed as he was by his constant desire to laugh. And all this flung him on Henia like on a bitch in heat, he burned for her and it really had nothing to do with love, no, it was something brutally humiliating which took place on an adolescent level—a childish love, in all its degradation. But at the same time it was not love—he really treated her like a young lady he had known "since he was a child," their conversation was free and familiar. "What's wrong with your hand?" "I scratched it opening a tin." "You know that Roblecki's gone to Warsaw?" And nothing else, not even a glance, just that. Who could suspect from this that there was anything between them? As for her, squeezed by the boy (if I may say so), and under his pressure, she had been violated in advance (if that makes sense), and, without losing her virginity, rendered on the contrary even more virginal by her partner, she was linked with him in the dark corners of his youthful, insufficiently manly compulsion. It could be said about her not that she "knew men" (as it is said about women of loose morals) but that she "knew the boy"—which was both innocent and infinitely more debauched. So it seemed, as they ate their noodles. They ate their noodles like a couple who have known each other since they were children, used to being together, and even a trifle bored. What? How could I hope Frederick would understand this, if the whole story were only a disgraceful illusion of mine? And so the day went by. Twilight. Dinner was served. We gathered once more at table in the dim light of the single oil lamp, the shutters closed, the doors bolted, and we ate curdled milk and potatoes; Henia's mother grazed the ring of her table napkin with her fingertips, Hippo turned his bloated face to the lamp. There was silence—but beyond the walls that protected us was the garden with its furtive and mysterious noises, and beyond the garden stretched the fields, fiercely ravaged by the war. . . The conversation came to an end and, sitting motionless, we watched a moth bumping into the glass of the lamp. In a dark corner of the room Karol was taking a lantern to pieces and cleaning it. Suddenly Henia bent over to bite through her thread—she was stitching a blouse—and this brisk movement and the bite were enough to cause Karol to blossom out and light up, in his corner, although he did not flinch. But she put her blouse aside and leaned her arm on the table, and this arm, in full view, correct, modest, even scholarly, belonging to her Mama and Papa—was at the same time bare, completely naked, yes, naked not with the nudity of an arm but of a knee peeping out from under a dress. . . of a leg. . . and, with this shameless and scholarly arm she needled him, teased him in an "idiotically youthful" way (it can hardly be given any other name), but at the same time in a brutal way. And this brutality was joined by a low, fascinating chant, which resounded in them or around them. Karol was cleaning the lantern. Henia did not budge. Frederick was rolling bread crumbs.

The bolted door of the veranda—the shutters reinforced with iron bars—our silence around the lamp, the table, increased by the threat of the outer elements—the objects, the clock, the cupboard, the shelf, seemed to be living a life of their own—in this silence, this heat, their precocious sensuality grew desperate, bloated with instinct and nocturnal, within a closed sphere of excitement and desire, a sort of magic circle. So much so that it looked as though they wanted to stir up through the night that other savage passion which roamed across the fields outside, so thirsty were they for violence. . . although they were serene and even sleepy. Frederick slowly extinguished his cigarette in the glass saucer of the cup of tea he had only half drunk, he extinguished it without hurrying, but a dog suddenly barked in the yard and his hand crushed the stub. Hippolytus' wife passed her slender fingers over her delicate hands, gently, as one picks an autumn leaf, as one smells a faded flower. Henia moved. . . so did Karol, by chance. . . this involuntary movement which bound them to each other sprang up like a flame, set them alight, and her white knees immediately threw (the boy) on his knees, his dark immobile knees, in the dark corner. Hippolytus' large, red, hairy hands, filled with flesh and antediluvian, lay on the tablecloth too, and Hippolytus had to put up with them, since they belonged to him.

"Let's go to bed," he yawned. And he murmured: "Let's go to bed."

No, it was really unbearable! Nothing, absolutely nothing! Nothing but my pornography by which to feast on them! And my fury with their unfathomable stupidity— this little fool, this stupid little goose—because stupidity was the only reason I could give for there being nothing, nothing whatsoever between them! . . . Ah, had they but been two or three years older! But Karol was sitting in his corner, with his lantern, with his childish hands and feet— and had nothing to do but repair his lantern, immersed in his work, turning the screws—and so much the worse if the greatest happiness were concealed in this adolescent god! . . . he turned the screws. And Henia drowsing at the table with bored arms. . . Nothing! It was unbelievable! And Frederick, what did Frederick know about it, extinguishing his cigarette, rolling bread crumbs? Frederick, Frederick, Frederick? Frederick, sitting at the table, at this table, in this house, among those nocturnal fields, in the middle of this knot of passion! With his face which was in itself an immense provocation, so careful was he not to appear provocative. Frederick!

Henia could hardly keep her eyes open. She said good

night. Shortly after Karol did the same thing and, carefully gathering his screws in a piece of paper, he went up to his room on the first floor.

I then tried to slip in guardedly, as I watched the lamp and its kingdom of buzzing satellites: "What a sweet couple!"

Nobody answered. Henia's mother touched her napkin with the tips of her fingers. "If God is willing," she said, "Henia will be getting engaged one of these days."

Frederick, still rolling bread crumbs, asked with polite interest:

"Oh yes? With someone in the neighborhood?"

"Yes, indeed. . . A neighbor. Young Paszkowski from Ruda. Not far from here. He often comes to see us. A very respectable young man. Very respectable. . ." She fluttered her eyelashes.

"A jurist, you know," Hippolytus brightened up. "He was going to buy a practice just before the war broke out. . . Intelligent, serious, a good brain, you know, a well-educated fellow! His mother's a widow, she manages the estate, twelve hundred acres of splendid land, twenty miles away."

"A saintly woman."

"She comes from near Lwow. She's a Trzeszewska, related to the Goluchowskis."

"Henia's still rather young. . . but she'll never make a better match. The boy's responsible, gifted, exceptionally intelligent. When he's here you'll have someone to talk to, that's all I'll say about him."

"But he's really very serious. Honest and upstanding. With a high moral code. The image of his mother. An extraordinary woman, deeply devout and religious. . . a saint. Ruda is a moral sanctuary."

"At least he's a gentleman. We know what he is and who he is."

"At least we know whom we're giving our daughter to."

"Thank God for that!"

"Whatever happens, Henia will make a good marriage. Whatever happens. . ." he added to himself, suddenly deep in thought.

4

The night passed smoothly and imperceptibly. Fortunately
I had a room to myself so I did not have to bear his sleep. . .
The open shutters disclosed a radiant morning with clouds
racing over the bluish garden soaked in dew, and the low
sun cast slanting rays which seemed to implicate everything
in their slant—the horse slanted, the tree slanted! Amusing!
Most amusing and witty! The horizontal surfaces were
vertical and the vertical surfaces slanting! This morning I
was feverish, almost ill as a result of the excitement of the
day before, of that fire and that glow—because it must be
understood that all this suddenly happened to me after
stifling, gray years of horror and exhaustion, or of insane
extravagance. During which I had almost forgotten what
beauty was. During which I had smelt nothing but the rank
stench of death. And now suddenly there appeared before
me the possibility of a warm idyll in a spring I thought
irrevocably ended, and disgust gave way to the marvelous
appetite of these two young people. I wanted nothing more.
I had had enough of this agony. I, a Polish writer, I, Gom-
browicz, chased after this will-o'-the-wisp as a fish chases its
bait—but what could Frederick know? The need to ascertain became unbearable, I had to know what he knew, what
he thought, what he imagined. I could no longer do without him, or rather I could no longer bear to be with him,

41

impenetrable as he was. Ask him? But how could I ask him? How could I put it? No, it was better to leave him to himself and watch him—he would soon end up by betraying his excitement. The opportunity presented itself after tea, as we were both sitting on the veranda: I stifled a yawn, I said I was going to have a short rest, and, on my way in, I hid behind the drawing room curtains. For that I required a certain amount of. . . courage. . . no, of audacity. . . because it looked rather like a provocation—but since there was something so provocative about him my act was no more than a way of "provoking the provoker." For me to hide behind the curtains put the first definite strain on our friendship and started a new, slightly illicit phase in our relationship.

What was more, every time I looked at him at moments when, absorbed by something else, he made no response to my gaze, I felt as though I had been caught doing something base. And yet I did not hesitate to hide behind the drawing room curtains. For some time he remained in the position I had left him in, sitting on the bench, his legs outstretched. He was gazing at the trees.

He moved. He stood up. He started to walk slowly around the courtyard, and he must have gone around it at least three times. . . before turning down under an arbor leading from the park to the orchard. I followed him at a distance, keeping him in sight. And I already felt I was on the right track.

Because Henia was in the orchard, peeling potatoes—was that where he was going? No. He went down a side path that led to the pond, and stood by the water, staring into space, his face that of a guest, of a tourist. . . Was his walk no more than a walk? I was on the verge of returning, convinced I had been deceived by my imagination (I had an obscure feeling that this man must sense these things: if he had not noticed anything it meant there was nothing to notice), when I suddenly saw him retrace his steps and come back under the arbor. I followed him.

He walked slowly, stopping from time to time to examine a plant, his intelligent profile bent over the leaves in the most obstinate way. The park was silent. My suspicions evaporated once more, only one remained: was he deceiving himself? He seemed to be making too many moves, to be too agitated as he wandered through the garden.

I was not mistaken. He changed direction twice more, and finally went into the orchard, went a little further, stopped, yawned, looked around. . . she was there, a hundred yards away, near the cellar, peeling potatoes! Sitting astride a sack! He glanced at her vaguely.

He yawned. Oh, it was incredible. The masquerade! For whose benefit? Why? All these precautions. . . as though he did not allow himself to participate in what she was doing. . . while it was obvious that he had been circling around her, getting nearer and nearer to her! There. . . now he was off toward the house, no, he went into the fields, went further, stopped, looked around, as though he really were going for a walk. . . but then he set out in a wide arc which led him back to the farmyard, yes, there was no doubt about it, he was going straight to the farmyard. Seeing this I ran as fast as I could through the bushes to get to a comfortable lookout post behind a shed, and, as I hurried over the broken twigs, through the bushes and across the ditch where a dead cat had been thrown and frogs hopped about, I realized that I was drawing the bushes and the ditch into our sinister game. I ran behind the shed. He was there, hidden by a wagon being loaded with manure. The horses suddenly stepped forward and he saw Karol in the opposite corner of the yard, examining a piece of iron near a shed.

It was then that he betrayed himself. Without the wagon

to screen him, unable to bear this open space between himself and the object of his curiosity, instead of remaining
where he stood, he rushed to a hedge so that the boy should
not see him, jumped over it, and stopped breathlessly. But
this sudden move had unmasked him—he was frightened,
and walked rapidly to the path leading to the house. Here,
he came across me. We were walking toward each other.

There was no way of avoiding the encounter. I had caught
him red-handed, and he had caught me. He had seen the
voyeur. We were making straight for each other, and I must
admit that I was by no means reassured, because now something was bound to change between us. I knew he knew, he
knew I knew he knew—this was what went through my
mind. We were still fairly far from each other when he
shouted:

"Well, my dear Witold, have you come out for a breath
of air?"

It was fearfully theatrical; that "Well, my dear Witold"
sounded terribly false. He never spoke to me like that. I
replied apathetically:

"Yes indeed. . . "

He took me by the arm—something he had never done
before—and suggested, just as jovially:

"What a glorious evening, how good the trees smell! May
I join you in your evening stroll?"

I replied, joining his contagious minuet:

"But of course, I'd be delighted!"

We went toward the house. But we no longer walked as
we walked normally. . . it was as though we had returned to
the park in another incarnation, ceremoniously, to the
sound of music. . . and I suspected he had taken some decision which held me in its claws. What had happened? For
the first time I felt he was hostile, menacing toward me. He
still held my arm, but his proximity had something cynical

and cold about it. We passed the house (he went on raving about the color scheme of the sunset) and I realized that we were taking the shortest way, straight across the lawn, to her. . . to the girl. . . and indeed the park, filled with rays and shadows, was like an immense bouquet, a blazing lamp bristling with firs and pine trees. We were walking toward her. She looked at us. She was still sitting on the sack, holding a knife. Frederick asked:

"Are we disturbing you?"

"Not at all. I've almost finished the potatoes."

He bent down and asked bluntly:

"May we invite the enchanting young lady to join us in our evening stroll?"

She got up and took off her apron. This eagerness. . . which may only have been politeness. After all, it was just a perfectly ordinary invitation to take a stroll in the garden, maybe said a little too emphatically, with the air of an old bachelor. . . but. . . but in this very approach, in this way of addressing her, I sensed an element of such shamelessness that I could not help thinking "he's going off to do things to her" or "she's going off with him to let him do things to her."

We took the shortest cut, across the lawn, to the farmyard, and she asked: "Are we going to see the horses?". . . His goal, his mysterious intent, seemed inscribed in the knowing pattern of the paths and lanes, the trees and the lawn. He did not reply. And this refusal to tell her where we were going filled me with fresh suspicions. A child. . . she was only a sixteen-year-old child. . . But we had almost reached the farmyard, with its floor of trodden earth, surrounded by the stables, the barn, the sheds, the watering-trough and a row of maples with the tips of the wagon shafts poking out behind them. . . she was a child, a child. . . but down there, by the shed, was another child, just as young, talking to the cartwright, still holding his piece of iron, standing near a heap of planks, beams, and sawdust, a wagon loaded with sacks, and the smell of chopped straw. We went nearer. Across the slope of trodden earth. When we got there, the three of us stopped.

The sun was setting and there was a curious sort of visibility which both confused and defined the objects—in this lighting a tree trunk, a hole in the bushes, the broken contour of a roof became clear in itself, visible in every detail. The dark-brown earth of the farmyard stretched up to the sheds. Karol was having a leisurely chat with the cartwright, like a peasant, leaning negligently against one of the posts supporting the roof of the shed and he did not interrupt his conversation when he saw us. We both stood there, with Henia between us, and it looked as though we had brought her to him—all the more so since neither of us spoke a word. Henia, too, was silent. . . and her silence expressed her shame. He put down his piece of iron and came up to us, but we did not know whom he was coming up to, to us or to Henia—and this gave him a certain duality, a certain awkwardness which threw him for an instant out of focus, but he joined us with ease, even with a certain gaiety. And yet the silence, because of our common awkwardness, lasted for a few seconds. . . and that was enough for stifling despair, regret, and all the nostalgia of Fate and Destiny to swoop down on them like a oppressive nightmare-ridden dream.

The languor, the beauty of the slim figure before us— what could produce them, apart from the fact that he was no man? Because we brought him Henia as a woman is brought to a man, but he was not one yet. . . he was not a man. He was no lord. No master. And he could not possess. Nothing could belong to him, he had no right to anything, he still had to serve, to obey—his fragility, his flexibility were even more accentuated in this farmyard, among the planks and the beams, and she responded to him in the same way: with fragility and flexibility. They were suddenly united, not like a man and a woman, but in another way, in a common offering to an unknown Moloch, incapable of possessing each other, only capable of offering themselves—and the sexual contract between them grew blurred, giving way to another contract, something undoubtedly more cruel but more beautiful. All that only lasted a few seconds. Nothing happened, either; all four of us just stood there. Frederick pointed to Karol's trousers which were slightly too long and dragged on the ground, and said:

"You ought to turn them up."

"That's true," said Karol. He bent down. Frederick said: "Just a minute."

It was obvious that what he had to say was not easy. He turned away slightly so as not to face them and, looking straight ahead, said in a hoarse but clear voice:

"No, wait. She can do it."

He repeated:

"She can do it."

The shamelessness of this demand—this breach made in their lives—was the admission of the excitement he required: do that, it'll excite me, that's what I want. . . That was how he introduced them to our lust, to the longing we nurtured for them. For half a second their silence quivered. And for half a second I waited for the result of Frederick's audacity. What followed was so simple and easy, yes, "easy," that I felt as dizzy as if an abyss had suddenly appeared before me.

She said nothing. She bent down and turned up his trousers. He had not even moved. Their silence was absolute.

I was suddenly overcome by the strange bareness of this

farmyard, with the shafts of the rack-wagons pointing at the sky, the broken drinking trough, the freshly thatched barn shining like a spark against the black, trodden earth and the woodpiles.

Frederick said: "Come on!" And we went toward the house—he, Henia and I. The audacity seemed still more obvious. Since we left almost immediately our presence near the shed meant one thing only: we had come so that she could turn up his trousers and now we were going away, Frederick, myself, and she. The house came into view with its windows, its double row of windows, below and above, and its veranda. We walked in silence.

We heard someone running across the lawn behind us, Karol caught us up and joined us. . . Still out of breath, he immediately fell into step with us: he walked along next to us, calmly and quietly. This hot race toward us was full of enthusiasm—he enjoyed our games, he wanted to join in— and his sudden change from a run into the calm pace of our return proved that he was aware of the necessity of discretion. All around could be felt the disintegration of being that invariably comes with the night. We gradually entered the dusk—Frederick, myself, Henia, Karol—like a curious erotic combination, a strange, sensual quartet.

5

How did it happen? I wondered, as I lay on a blanket on the cool grass, breathing in the humidity of the earth. How did it happen? She turned up his trousers? Very well. She did it because she could do it, of course, just as a simple favor. . . but she knew what she was doing. She knew it was for Frederick—for his pleasure—so she was prepared to let him extract pleasure from her. . . From her, but not from her alone. . . From her and from Karol. So that was it! She knew that they could both excite and seduce. . . Frederick, at least. . . and Karol knew too, since he had joined in the game. . . In that case they were not as stupid as we thought! They were conscious of their flavor! And if they were conscious of it in spite of their inexperienced youth, it is youth that has far greater intuition for these things than the age of maturity; in a way they were professionals, they possessed the infallible instinct of their premature flesh, their premature blood, their premature tastes. I was the bungler of the piece, not they. But then why did they behave like children in their own relationship? So innocently? If they ceased being innocent the minute a third actor appeared on the stage? If they behaved with such subtlety toward him? What worried me most of all was that this third actor should be none other than Frederick, who was normally so prudent, so level-headed! This sudden march across the

park, this defiant advance, like a military maneuver, this
march which was to offer the girl to the boy! What was it?
What did it mean? Was I not responsible for it all? Having spied on him I had revealed his secret folly, he had been
surprised, caught out in his mystery—and now the beast of
his secret dream had escaped from its cage and, together
with my beast, could rage at will! At the moment the situation was such that all four of us were the mute accomplices
in an inadmissible crime, which excluded any explanation
in advance, which smothered us with shame.

Her, his—their knees, four knees, in trousers, in a skirt,
and (young). . . In the afternoon the famous Albert Paszkowski we had spoken about the day before arrived. A handsome man! Well-built and elegant, no doubt about it!
With a prominent but fine nose, very mobile nostrils, eyes
like olives and a deep voice—and under his sensitive nose
his well-clipped mustache reclined on full, red lips. The sort
of manly good looks that appeal to women. . . because
women admire a fine figure just as much as the aristocratic
delicacy of the details, like the thin veins of the hands with
long fingers and well-manicured nails. Who could question
his well-bred foot with its high instep, encased in an elegant,
yellow shoe, or his small, well-formed ears? Were they not
interesting and even, I might say, seductive, those little pits
in his forehead which made him seem so intellectual? And
was his pale complexion not that of a minstrel? Unques-
tionably a handsome gentleman! A victorious jurist! A distinguished lawyer! I hated him from the first, with a hatred
mingled with disgust of a totally unjustifiable violence
which amazed me—because he was charming and *comme il
faut*. In fact it was neither loyal nor fair to resent the small
imperfections, like, for instance, a slight swelling and fullness which rested lightly on his cheeks and his fingers,
which lurked in the region of his stomach, and which was

also highly distinguished. Maybe I was annoyed by the excessive and rather sensual subtlety of his features, of his mouth all too eager to eat, of his nose all too ready to smell, of his fingers all too prepared to feel—and yet all this made him a lover! What must have repelled me in him was the impossibility of nakedness—because his body needed a collar, studs, a handkerchief, and even a hat; it was a body in shoes, which called for toilet requisites and garments. . . but the worst thing of all was the transformation of certain defects, like the incipient baldness and the soft corpulence, into attributes of elegance and distinction. The physical appearance of a peasant has the immense advantage that the peasant pays no attention to it, so that it never shocks even if it be anti-aesthetic—but a man who dresses with care emphasizes his physical appearance, enjoys it and revels in it, so that every defect becomes lethal. But why had I suddenly developed such sensitivity about somebody else's body? Why this disgraceful passion for spying on people?

And yet I must admit that the newcomer behaved with intelligence and even with a certain amount of distinction. He did not give himself airs, spoke little and not too loudly. He was very polite. His politeness, his modesty, were the result of a good education, but must also have been innate: his character, by no means frivolous, was reflected in his eyes which seemed to say: I respect you, respect me too. No, he was not at all self-satisfied. He was aware of his faults and would undoubtedly have liked to be different— but he was himself with as much ease, intelligence, and dignity as possible, and although he was soft and fragile looking, he must have been violently obstinate, even determined. His good manners certainly did not stem from his weakness but from a principle, probably a moral one, of duty toward others; at the same time his manners categorically affirmed his class and his highly personal style. He had probably resolved to defend his values: subtlety, delicacy, and sensitivity, and he defended them all the more violently since history was harrowing them pitilessly. His arrival caused a number of changes in our little world. Hippolytus, previously so cautious, seemed to have found a secure track along which to run, he stopped murmuring to himself, ceased his bitter observations, and it was as though he were allowed to take his elegant suits of times gone by out of the closet and wear them once more—he was once again the blustering, ingenuous, jovially hospitable squire. "Well, how's it going? What's new? Have some vodka, it'll do you good!" And his wife pirouetted in her pale languor, and, fluttering her slim fingers, she spread a veil of hospitality.

Frederick responded to the respect Albert displayed for him with an even deeper respect; he allowed him to pass before him into the drawing room, and it was only when Albert insisted that he consented, as a special favor, to enter the room first—it was like Versailles. Then began a real tournament of courtesies—but the strange thing was that each of them seemed to be taking himself into consideration and not the other. After the first words Albert realized that he was dealing with somebody exceptional, but he was far too worldly to show it—and yet the rank he ascribed to Frederick aroused his own self-esteem, he decided his behavior should be *à la hauteur* and treated himself with exquisite courtesy. Frederick assimilated this aristocratic state of mind with enthusiasm, and became overweeningly arrogant—occasionally condescending to participate in the conversation, but only so as not to inflict an undeserved punishment on his listeners by remaining persistently silent. His fear of being incorrect suddenly turned into superiority and pride! As for Henia (who was the real reason for the visit) and Karol, they were drained of all significance. Sit-

ing on a chair near the window she looked like a good little
girl, with him, her elder brother, watching his sister's courtship and furtively checking whether his hands were dirty.

What a meal! Pastries and cakes appeared on the table!
And then we went into the garden, where there was serenity
and sunshine. The young couple, Albert and Henia, preceded us. We followed them at a short distance so as not
to disturb them. . . Hippolytus and his wife, rather moved,
joking gently to each other, and next to them myself and
Frederick, who was telling me about Venice.

Albert must have been asking her something, explaining
something to her, as she tilted her head toward him, atten-
tive and devoted, waving a blade of grass in her hand.

Karol walked across the lawn on his own, like a brother
who is bored to tears by his sister's courtship and does not
know what to do next.

"It's like a stroll before the war," I told Maria, who replied with a wave of her hand. We were approaching the
pond.

But Karol's vagrancy became more nervous and more
obvious, he clearly did not know what to do and his movements, imbued with boredom, seemed impatiently restrained. And, at the same time, although we could not hear
them, all the things Henia was saying to Albert began to be
addressed to Karol—once again her whole existence was
surreptitiously united to (the boy), in spite of herself, because she never looked around and could not even have
known that Karol was with us. And this tender talk she
was having with Albert, as though they really were engaged,
underwent, because of (the boy) following them, a sudden
devaluation, while she herself began to radiate a kind of
perversity. The enamored jurist pulled a branch of haw-
thorn toward her so she could pick a spray of blossom, and
she seemed grateful, even touched; but this emotion did

not end with Albert, it continued to Karol and, as it reached him, became obstinately young and adolescent, idiotically undecided and indifferent. . . it was the disparagement of their love, devoid of its real weight, turned into a base and vulgar feeling, taking place on an inferior level, on the level of a sixteen-year-old girl and a seventeen-year-old boy, on the level of their inadequacy and their youth. We came around a clump of hazel trees at the edge of the pond, and there we saw an old woman.

She was doing her washing in the pond and when she saw us she turned and stared at us—an old woman, a broad-bottomed old slut with sagging breasts, hideous, rancid and foully decrepit, with evil little eyes. She watched us, holding her wooden beetle.

Karol broke away from us and walked up to her as though he had something to say to her. And then he suddenly pulled up her skirt. For a second we could see her white belly and the black patch of hair! She bellowed. The boy made an obscene gesture, turned on his heels and came back to us as though nothing had happened, while the old woman yelled at him.

We did not say a word. It was such an unexpected and blatant obscenity, and it had disturbed us brutally. . . But Karol was already ambling along next to us, as serene as ever. Albert and Henia, deep in conversation, had disappeared around a bend in the path—maybe they had not seen anything?—and we followed them in silence, Hippolytus, his wife a trifle disconcerted, Frederick. . . What? What had happened? It was not so much the prank that had upset me, it was the fact that it could be transformed on another level, in another mode, into a perfectly natural gesture, and that Karol should continue to stroll along next to us, as charming as ever, with the strange charm of a scoundrel who assaults old women, a charm that grew on

me without my being able to understand it. How could this
foul gesture crown him with such grace? He literally glowed
with this incomprehensible charm and Frederick patted me
on the shoulder and whispered, almost inaudibly:

"Well, well!"

But he immediately turned his exclamation into a well-
formulated sentence, which he pronounced loudly and
affectedly:

"Well, well, what have you got to say for yourself, my
dear Witold?"

I replied:

"Nothing. Nothing, my dear Frederick."

Maria turned to us.

"I'll show you a fine specimen of American thuya. I
planted it myself."

It was so as not to interrupt the young couple. We ex-
amined the thuya until a farm lad came running up, waving his arms. Hippolytus turned sharply: "What is it?"
"The Germans have come from Opatow!" Sure enough
there were some people standing by the stables. He immediately rushed over to them, apoplectically, his wife behind him, Frederick behind them, thinking he could help
them with his good knowledge of German. As for me, I did
not want to get involved with them, I suddenly felt exhausted by the idea of these inevitable, oppressive Germans. . . What a nightmare. . . I went back to the house.

The house was empty, the rooms deserted, the abandoned furniture seemed to exist with greater intensity. . . I
waited for the result of the Germans' visit, taking place
silently by the stables. . . but soon I was waiting for Albert
and Henia who had vanished around the bend in the path. . .
and suddenly the thought of Frederick exploded in this
abandoned house. Where was Frederick? With the Germans? Not so sure. . . Was it not more likely that he would

be elsewhere, by the pond, where he had left the girl? He was there! He must have been there! He had gone back to spy on them. And what did he see? I was jealous of whatever he could see. Cast out of the house by its very emptiness I ran out as though I were going to the farmyard where the Germans were, but in fact I made straight for the pond, through the bushes, along the ditch where the frogs hopped with revolting, fat splashes, I went around the pond and saw them—Albert and Henia—sitting on a bench at the edge of the garden, facing the meadow. Night was falling, it was nearly dark. The air was damp. Where was Frederick? It was impossible for him not to be here. I was not mistaken: down there, among the willows, in a hollow, barely perceptible, he was at his post under the bushes, staring at them. I did not hesitate. I crept up to him and stood next to him. He did not budge and, as I gazed, my silent appearance as a watchman made me a defiant accomplice of his! On the bench two silhouettes could be distinguished, they must have been talking to each other, but so softly that they could not be heard.

That was deceitful of (the girl)—appallingly deceitful—there she was, fawning on the lawyer while (the boy) to whom she should have been faithful had been banished far away from her. . . I could not bear this idea, it was as though the last possibility of beauty were disintegrating in the world that used to be mine, invaded from now on by decomposition, agony, torture, and horror. What a disgrace! Was he embracing her? Or was he holding her hand? What a disgusting and hateful receptacle his hands were for hers! Suddenly I felt, as one feels in a dream, on the point of making a discovery, and, looking around, I saw. . . I saw something astounding.

Frederick was not alone: next to him, a few steps away, hidden in the bushes, was Karol.

Karol there? Next to Frederick? But how had Frederick managed to get him there? On what pretext? Whatever it was, he was there and I knew he was there for Frederick and not for her—he had not come to spy on what was happening on the bench, he had been attracted by Frederick's presence. It was as indistinct as it was subtle, and I do not know how to put it. . . I had the impression that (the boy) had come without being invited, only to arouse us. . . to emphasize. . . to make our feelings more agonizing. No doubt, while the other man, the adult stood staring at the child, shattered by her deceit, he, the little boy, had silently stolen out of the bushes and stood next to him without saying a word. It was bold and savage! But night was falling, we were almost invisible and perfectly silent—none of us could say a thing. The unlikely cynicism of our act foundered in the vacuity of the night and the silence. What was more, the presence of (the boy) effaced it, almost forgave us; his lightness, his slimness absolved us and he, so (youthfully) attractive, could join anybody he liked. . . (later I shall explain the meaning of these parentheses). . . And suddenly he went away as easily as he had arrived.

But the fact that he should have joined us like a shadow now made the sight of the bench pierce us like a dagger. This fantastic, wild apparition of (the boy) while (the girl) deceived him! All situations in the world are figures. The appallingly significant events that had happened here could not be understood or fully deciphered. The world was pitching in an unexpected way. And then, from the stables, we heard a shot. We rushed toward the farmyard, all of us together. Albert running next to me, Henia next to Frederick. Frederick, always level-headed and resourceful in moments of crisis, cut behind the shed, and we followed him. What we saw was by no means so bad. A slightly tipsy German was shooting pigeons with a double-barreled gun. Anyhow, they soon got into their truck and drove off, waving us good-by. Hippolytus looked at us in fury.

"Leave me alone!"

His eyes popped out of him like out of a window, but he closed all the doors and windows immediately. He went into the house.

That evening at dinner, ruddy and serene, he poured us out some vodka.

"Well? Let's drink to Albert and Henia. They're getting engaged."

Frederick and I congratulated them.

6

Alcohol. Vodka. An intoxicating episode. An episode like
a large glass of alcohol—and then another glass—but this
drunkenness was a steep slope, and at every moment there
was the danger of toppling into filth and corruption, into a
sensual quagmire. But how could one refrain from drinking? Drink had become a nutriment, everybody drank however he could and whenever he could—and so did I. I
simply endeavored to rescue my dignity and retain, in my
drunkenness, the appearance of a scholar who continues his
researches in spite of everything, who gets drunk in order
to study. And so I studied.

Albert left after breakfast. It was agreed that we should
all go to Ruda the next day.

Karol drove the break up to the front door. He was off
to Ostrowiec to get some paraffin oil. I offered to go with
him.

Frederick was opening his mouth to make the same suggestion—when he was suddenly overcome by one of those
feelings of embarrassment. . . to which he was liable at any
moment. He was opening his mouth, but he shut it, opened
it once more and remained in the grip of this agonizing
game as Karol and I drove off in the break.

The cruppers of the horses as they trotted, the sandy
path, the wide horizons, the slow whirl of the hills rising

above each other into the distance. . . The early morning, out in the open, he and I, myself next to him, both of us emerging from the Poworna valley, exposed to view, and my incongruous presence next to him, visible for miles around.

I started off by saying: "Well, Karol, why did you do what you did to that old woman last night by the pond?"

To have a more specific idea of my question he asked, rather suspiciously:

"What?"

"Everybody saw you!"

This was a vague prelude—just a means of beginning a conversation. He laughed, just in case, and also to put what we said in a lighter vein. "Why shouldn't I?" he said, and cracked his whip, indifferently. . . I told him how surprised I was: "If only she'd been pretty! But an old slut like that!" Since he did not answer I went on: "Do you like old women?"

He nonchalantly thrashed his whip at a plant on the side of the road. And as though that were the reply to my questions he lashed out at the horses which plunged forward and almost upset the break. I understood the answer, although it could not be put into words. For a while we drove on at a faster pace. Then the horses slowed down and he grinned, revealing his white teeth, and said:

"What does it matter whether they're young or old?"

And he roared with laughter.

That worried me. I shuddered. I was sitting next to him. What did that mean? To begin with one thing struck me: the extraordinary importance of his white teeth which gleamed and frolicked within him, his inner, purifying whiteness. His teeth far more important than his words—he seemed to speak for the sole benefit of his teeth —and he could say anything because he spoke for pleasure, devoted to his game and his joy, and he knew that his joyous teeth would be forgiven the foulest obscenities. Who was sitting next to me? Someone like me? Not at all: a being essentially different from myself, an enchanting being from a heavenly realm, endowed with a grace which was gradually turning into charm. A prince and a poem. But why did this prince assault an old woman? That was the question. And why did he enjoy it? Did he enjoy his own lust? Did he enjoy the fact that, being a prince, he was at the mercy of an appetite that made him lust after the most hideous of women? Did this Adonis (Henia's partner) think so little of himself that he did not care who satisfied him, nor whom he mixed with? Here there was something obscure. We went down the hill. In him I found sacrilege resulting from lightheartedness, sacrilege with which the spirit was involved, which contained an element of despair.

(Maybe I only indulged in these speculations so that I could retain the appearance of a scholar at this feast.)

Had he pulled up the old woman's skirt so as to behave like a soldier? Was that not the sort of thing a soldier would do?

Changing the subject—because I began to fear for myself—I inquired: "Why do you have such rows with your father?" He hesitated, puzzled, but realized that I must have found out from Hippolytus. He replied:

"Because he's always pestering my mother. He never leaves her in peace, the swine. If he weren't my father I'd. . ."

A perfectly normal answer—he could confess his love for his mother by admitting he hated his father and avoid any sentimentality—but I decided to pin him down and asked him bluntly: "Do you love your mother very much?"

"Of course! She's my mother. . . ."

Which meant there was nothing strange about it since
it is perfectly normal for a boy to love his mother. And yet
this intrigued me. At close quarters it seemed odd: a minute ago he had been a pure anarchist who assaulted an old
woman, and now he had become conventional, submitting
to the law of filial love. Which did he believe in—anarchy
or law? If he submitted so passively to convention it was
not to increase but to detract from his own value, and to
make his love for his mother perfectly commonplace and
unimportant. Why did he always underrate himself? This
idea was curiously attractive: why did he love to disparage
himself? This idea was pure alcohol. . . why, with him,
was every idea either fascinating or repulsive, always passionate and intense? We had passed Grocholice and we
drove uphill, past a yellow earth wall in which cellars for
storing potatoes had been dug. The horses were walking—
and there was silence. Karol suddenly brightened up:
"Couldn't you get me a job in Warsaw? In the black mar-
ket, for instance? I'd be able to give my mother a hand if
I were earning some money, because she has to take a cure.
And now my father's always grumbling because I haven't
got a job. I'm fed up with the whole thing!" Now he could
really talk, because it was about material and practical matters; it was also perfectly natural for him to talk about them
to me. . . or was it so natural? Was it not just an excuse
for making contact with me, the adult, for coming closer to
me? Of course, at such a difficult time, a boy had to rely
on older people, more powerful than himself, and could
only hope to gain their good will through personal
charm. . . But the coquetry of a young man is infinitely
more complicated than that of a girl, who always has the advantage of her sex. . . So, this was probably calculated,
however unconsciously, oh, and innocently! He was turning
to me for help, but in fact he really did not care about a

job in Warsaw, he simply wanted attention, he wanted to break the ice. . . the rest would follow on its own. . . Break the ice? But how? And what was "the rest" that would follow? I only knew, or rather suspected that his adolescence wanted to come into contact with my maturity. I also knew that he was not spoiled and that his appetite, his lust, made him easily accessible. . . I winced when I sensed his secret longing to come closer to me. . . as though that whole world of his were going to invade me. I do not know if I am making myself clear. The relationship between an adult and a boy usually takes place on a level of technical matters, of assistance and collaboration; but the minute it becomes more intimate its faintly improper nature reveals itself. I felt that this individual was going to seduce me with his youth, and it was as though I, the adult, were going to be irrevocably compromised.

But to use the word "youth"—that is to confound him.

We reached the top of the hill and were confronted with the unaltered view: the earth rising in hills, swollen in a motionless surge in the slanting light which here and there pierced the clouds.

"It's better if you stay with your parents. . . " That sounded categorical because I spoke as an adult, and that enabled me to extend our conversation by asking: "Do you like Henia?"

The most difficult question of all had slipped out with no difficulty, and with the same ease he replied:

"Of course I like her."

Pointing with his whip he added: "You see those bushes over there? They're not bushes, they're the tops of trees in the valley of Lisin, which leads to the Bodzechow forests. That's where some of the gangs go and hide, sometimes. . . " He gave me a conspiratorial wink. We drove along the road, past a crucifix on the right, and I went on as though I had not left off. . . A sudden tranquillity, which I could not account for, enabled me to ignore the time that had elapsed:

"But you're not in love with her?"

This question was far more hazardous, it approached the heart of the matter, and, in its very insistence, could betray my somber emotions, mine and Frederick's, which had been conceived at their feet, at their feet, at their feet. . . I felt as though I were arousing a sleeping tiger. But without reason.

"Nooo. . . we've known each other since we were children! . . . " and it was said without any *arrière-pensée*. . . and yet one would have expected the episode by the shed, in which we had all been accomplices, to have made it slightly more difficult to reply.

Not at all! For him the episode must have been on another level—and now he felt no connection with it—his drawled "Nooo" had the flavor of an irresponsible caprice, even of banter. He spat. By spitting he completed his transformation into a bantering little scamp and he immediately laughed with that disarming laugh which seemed to dispense with the possibility of any other reaction; he looked at me out of the corner of his eye, and leered:

"I'd rather have the mother. . . "

No! It could not be true! Hippolytus' wife with her tearful thinness? Then why did he say it? Because he had pulled up the old woman's skirt? But then why had he pulled it up? How absurd! What an insoluble riddle! And yet I knew (and it was one of the basic principles of my literary science of man) that there are certain human deeds which seem totally senseless, but which are necessary for man because they define him. A simple example of that is the man who is prepared, for no apparent reason, to commit the wildest of follies, simply so as not to feel a coward.

And surely the young, more than anyone else, feel this need to define themselves in this particular way? . . . It was more than likely, even certain, that most of the words and deeds of the adolescent sitting next to me, holding the reins and the whip, were, precisely, "self-tests"—and even our—Frederick's and my—secretive and enchanted glances must have encouraged him, without his knowing it, to play this game with himself. Very well: he went for a walk with us yesterday, was bored and had nothing to do, so he pulled up the old woman's skirt to do something lewd, which might at last change him from one who is desired to one who desires. Quite a little acrobat! All right. But why harp on it and pretend he would "rather" have the mother? Might it not conceal some secret, more aggressive intention?

"You're not going to make me believe that!" I said. "You'd rather the mother than the daughter? What nonsense!" I added. To which he obstinately replied, as the sun beat down: "But it's true."

Stuff and nonsense! But why, what was the point of it? We were nearly in Bodzechow and, in the distance, we could see the blast furnaces of the Ostrowiec steelworks. Why, why was he dismissing Henia, why did he not want her? I knew without knowing, I understood without understanding. Would his youth really prefer adults? Did he want to be "with adults?" What was this idea leading to? The unlikelihood, the burning keenness, the dramatic character of this idea soon put me on the right track, because in his strange world, I only believed in intuitions and impulses. Did this brat want to prevail in our maturity? It was perfectly normal for a boy to fall in love with a beautiful girl and for their love to take the course of a natural attraction, but maybe he wanted something. . . vaster, more daring. . . ? He did not want to be merely "a boy with a girl" but "a boy with adults," a boy who breaks into

maturity. . . What an obscene, perverse idea! Behind him
lay the experience of war and anarchy, I did not know him,
could not know him, I did not know what had formed
him or how, he was as puzzling as the landscape—familiar
and yet unfamiliar—there was only one thing I could be
sure about: that this scamp had been out of his swaddling
clothes for some time! To get involved with what? It was
impossible to tell—it was not clear whom or what he preferred. Maybe he wanted to amuse himself with us and not
with Henia, and was therefore trying to make me realize
that age was no obstacle. . . What? Yes, yes, he was bored,
he wanted to amuse himself, to amuse himself with a game
which he did not yet know, which he had never even
dreamed of—out of boredom, out of laziness, nonchalantly
—with us, and not with Henia, because we, in our ugliness,
could lead him further, we were more unbounded. And so
(recalling what had happened by the shed) he wanted me
to know that he was not shocked. All right. I was nauseated
by the idea that his beauty could search for my ugliness. I
changed the subject.

"Do you go to church? Do you believe in God?"

A question which called him to order, a question designed to shield me from his deceptive lightness.

"In God? Well, you know what the priests say. . ."

"But you do believe in God?"

"Of course. But. . ."

"But what?"

He said nothing.

I should have asked: "Do you go to church?" instead of
which I asked: "Do you sleep with women?"

"Sometimes."

"Are you successful with women?"

He laughed.

"No. How could I be? I'm far too young."

Too young. The meaning was humiliating—that was why he could use the word "young" deliberately. But as for me, who had just confused God with women, because of this boy, in some grotesque and almost drunken blunder, I sensed a curious admonition in this "too young." Yes, too young, too young for women, and for God, too young for everything—and what did it matter if he believed in God or not, if he was successful with women or not, because whatever happened he was "too young" and nothing he could do, say, or feel mattered: he was incomplete, he was "too young." He was "too young" for Henia and for all that happened between them, "too young" for Frederick as well, and for me. What was this fragile immaturity? It was meaningless, it did not count! How could I, as an adult, put all my gravity into his lack of gravity, listen to someone of no importance and tremble? I glanced at the countryside. From the top of the hill we could already see the bed of the Kamienna, and even hear the distant rattle of a train coming into Bodzechow; the entire valley lay before us, with the main road winding through it, and right and left the green and yellow chessboard of fields stretching into the distance—a sleepy eternity, but gagged, stifled, throttled. An oppressive smell of iniquity permeated this landscape and, in this iniquity, myself with this boy who was "too young," too light, too flighty, whose insufficiency, whose incompletion were being transformed into an elementary power. . . How could I defend myself against him if I could find no support in anything?

We drove onto the main road and the metal-rimmed wheels of the break clattered over the potholes; the road filled with people and we drove past them as they appeared on the pavement, one in a cap, another in a hat; a little further on we passed a wagon full of bundles, the possessions of an entire family, which a horse dragged along; still further on a woman stopped us; she was standing in the middle of the road and came up to us: I saw a fine face under a rustic kerchief, enormous feet in a man's boots below a rather short, black, silk dress and a low, elegant décolleté like that of an evening gown: she held a parcel wrapped in a newspaper—she had waved to us with it— she wanted to say something, but pursed her lips, then wanted to speak again, but gave a disillusioned wave of her hand, stepped back and stood motionless, watching us move away. Karol sniggered. We finally drove into Ostrowiec, making a terrible din, jolting over the cobbles with our cheeks quivering; we drove past the German sentries in front of the factory; the town had not changed, it was just as it had been, the same squat factory buildings and the blast furnace chimneys, the wall, the bridge on the Kamienna and the crisscross of rails, and the main road leading to the square with the Café Malinowski on the corner. And yet something was missing—there were no Jews. But the streets were crowded, even lively; a woman was sweeping her doorstep, a man was carrying a huge bundle of ropes, a group of people stood in front of a grocery, a street urchin aimed a stone at a sparrow perched on a chimney top. We took a full load of paraffin oil, did some shopping, and left this curiously inhospitable town as quickly as we could. We heaved a sigh of relief as the break drove off the main road, onto the soft soil of the lane. But what was Frederick doing? Was he asleep? Was he sitting down? Was he going for a walk? I knew how scrupulously correct he always was, I was certain that if he were sitting down it would be with all due precautions, and yet I began to suffer from the uncertainty I felt about the way he was spending his time. He was not there when Karol and I returned and sat down to a late lunch; Hippolytus' wife told me he was raking. . . What, for Heaven's sake? He was raking a path in the garden. "I'm afraid he's rather bored here," she said, obviously distressed, as though he were a guest of before the war, and even Hippolytus came up to tell me:

"Your friend is in the garden, you know. . . He's raking."

And something in his voice told me that he was beginning to find this man's company slightly oppressive; he was ashamed, unhappy, and embarrassed. I went to look for Frederick. When he saw me he put down his rake and asked me with his customary politeness how our trip had gone. . . then, looking away, he suggested tentatively that we should return to Warsaw, because, after all, we were perfectly useless down here and, on the other hand, our business interests might suffer considerably if we neglected them for so long, yes, this journey had been undertaken too hastily, it might be better to pack our bags. . . He gradually made his way toward this decision which he had not yet taken, made it gradually more intense, tried to convince himself, to convince me, to convince the trees in the park. What did I think? On the one hand, of course, the country had its advantages. . . but. . . well, we might just as well leave the next day, mightn't we? Suddenly his questions became urgent and I understood: he wanted to know, from my answer, whether I had succeeded in getting anything out of Karol; he realised that I must have tried during the journey to Ostrowiec; he wanted to know if there were still the shadow of a hope that Albert's tender fiancée might end up in Karol's adolescent embrace! At the same time he wanted to tell me secretly that none of the things he knew about the matter entitled us to such an illusion.

It is hard to describe the humiliation of this scene. The true face of an elderly man is concealed by a secret will power, trying to mask the decay, or at least to arrange it in an attractive whole—once disappointment had set in Frederick lost all his charm, all hope and all passion, and his wrinkles spread and crawled over his face like worms on a corpse. He was abject, humbly odious in this submission to his own horror—and his abjection contaminated me to such an extent that my own worms arose, crawled out, climbed up, and polluted my face. But that was not the limit of the humiliation. The sinister comicality of this situation was mainly due to the fact that we were like a couple of lovers deceived and rejected by another couple: our passion, our excitement had nothing on which to feed, and now raged between us. . . We had nothing left except each other. . . and in spite of our revulsion we had to remain together in this sensuality which had been unleashed and was dragging us with it. So we tried not to look at each other. The sun beat down and the bushes smelt of cantharis.

At the end of this secret conference I realized what a blow for me and for him the indifference of those two had been, an indifference which now seemed beyond doubt. The girl—engaged to Albert. The boy—who did not care about it. And all this foundered in their youthful blindness. The ruin of all our dreams!

I told Frederick he was probably right, that our prolonged absence from Warsaw might really injure our business interests. He immediately clung to my agreement. The idea of flight prevailed, and, as we walked up the path, we accustomed ourselves to this decision.

But behind the corner of the house, on the pathway leading to the study, we saw them both. She was holding a bottle. He was standing in front of her. They were talking. Their childishness, their complete childishness was obvious and lethal: she—the schoolgirl, he—the schoolboy, the brat.

Frederick asked them: "What are you doing?"

She: "I've pushed the cork into the bottle."

Karol, holding the bottle up against the light: "I'll get it out with a piece of wire."

Frederick: "That's not so easy."

She: "Maybe I ought to get another cork."

Karol: "It's not worth it. . . I'll get it out. . . "

Frederick: "The neck's too narrow."

Karol: "If it went in it must come out."

She: "Or crumble and muck up the fruit juice."

Frederick did not answer. Karol shifted stupidly from one leg to the other. She stood there holding the bottle and said:

"I'll get some corks upstairs. There aren't any in the sideboard."

Karol: "I tell you I can get it out."

Frederick: "It won't be easy to force it through the neck."

She: "He that seeketh findeth."

Karol: "You know what? Those little bottles in the cupboard!"

She: "No. That's medicine."

Frederick: "You can wash them."

A bird flew by.

Frederick: "What sort of bird is that?"

Karol: "An oriole."

Frederick: "Are there many around here?"

She: "Look, what an enormous worm!"

Karol went on shifting from leg to leg, she raised her foot and scratched her calf—then he raised his shoe, turned it in a semicircle, resting it on the heel, and crushed the worm. . . but only half of it, because his toe did not reach any further and he was too lazy to move his heel; the rest of the worm started to twist and writhe feverishly while the boy gazed at it with interest. It would have been no more horrifying than the death of a fly on a piece of fly-paper, or of a moth on a lamp bulb, had it not been for Frederick's glassy stare, riveted on the worm, revealing its agony to the full. He could have looked indignant but in fact he only wanted to identify himself with the torture, to drain the cup to the dregs. He took the agony on himself, sucked it in, gorged himself on it, and, sluggish and dumb in the grip of the vice, he could no longer move. Karol looked at him out of the corner of his eye, without dispatching the worm; Frederick's horror seemed quite hysterical.

Henia moved her slipper and it was she who crushed the worm.

But only the other end of it, deliberately sparing the middle so it could go on twisting and writhing in pain.

All that was—meaningless. . . as only crushing a worm can be meaningless.

Karol: "There are masses of birds around Lwow."

Henia: "I've got some more potatoes to peel."

Frederick: "I don't envy you. . . it's a terrible bore. . . "

As we returned to the house we continued our conversation, then Frederick disappeared—I do not know where—but I knew what he was doing. He was thinking about what had just happened, about the two innocent legs which had united over the writhing body, in a common act of cruelty. Cruelty? Was it really cruelty? It was more like a trifle: they stepped on a worm, for no reason, casually, just because it was there—how many worms does one kill every day? No, no, it was not cruelty—it was thoughtlessness: gazing childishly at entertaining death throes, without feeling any pain. What did it matter to them? But for Frederick? For a mind accustomed to getting to the heart of a matter? For his extreme sensitivity? For him this act

was surely horrifying enough to make his blood run cold?
—because suffering is as distressing in the body of a worm
as it is in the body of a giant, suffering is "one," in the
same way that space is "one," it is indivisible and every-
time it appears it is abomination itself. They had caused
suffering, created pain, with the soles of their shoes they
had transformed the peaceful existence of this worm into
something abominable, an inferno—it was impossible to
imagine a greater crime, a greater sin. Sin. . . sin. . . Yes,
it was a sin, but if it was a sin it was a common sin. . . their
legs had united on the writhing body of the worm. . .

I knew what he was thinking, the lunatic! The lunatic!
He was thinking about them—he thought they had done
it "for him." "Don't deceive yourself. Don't think we
haven't got anything in common. . . You saw what happened: one of us crushed a worm. . . And then the other
one joined in. We did it for you. To be united—before
you and for you—in sin."

That must have been what Frederick was thinking. Or
maybe I was only attributing my thoughts to him? And
maybe he was attributing his thoughts to me. . . thinking
no more about me than I was about him. . . so that each
of us was lovingly cultivating his thought, but in the other
one's mind. This amused me, I laughed aloud, and I
thought that he must be laughing too. . .

"We did it for you. To be united before you and for you
in sin. . . "

If this were really the content of the secret message
they wanted to transmit to us with their unconsciously
cruel legs. . . then they had no need to repeat it! A word
to the wise! I smiled again at the idea that Frederick was
perhaps smiling at this moment as he thought of what I
thought of him, and what I thought was this: that he had
given up his assiduously formed plans to leave, and that

he was again like a bloodhound on a trail, excited by freshly aroused hopes.

The hopes, the perspectives hidden in this little word "sin," were colossal. If these children were really tempted to sin. . . with each other. . . but also with us. . . Ah, I could almost see Frederick meditating somewhere, his head in his hands, thinking that sin penetrates to our heart of hearts, that it rivets people to each other as firmly as the most passionate caress, that sin, private, secret, and disgraceful, allows us to penetrate as deeply into the existence of others as the sexual act allows us to penetrate their bodies. If this were so. . . it meant that he, Frederick ("that he, Witold," thought Frederick). . . that both of us were not too old for those two—in other words that their youth was accessible. There was this common sin: a sin which was almost created to join in illegal matrimony the flowering of the young couple to somebody—somebody not so attractive. . . somebody older and more serious. In virtue they were hermetically sealed to us. But once in sin they could wallow in it with us. . . that was what Frederick was thinking! And I could almost see him, his finger on his mouth, meditating, searching for the sin that would enable him to penetrate them, reviewing every sin imaginable to find the right one—or else thinking, suspecting that I was searching for a similar sin. What a marvelous system of mirrors: he was reflected in me, I was reflected in him—and so, as we wove dreams for each other we came to conclusions which neither of us wanted to admit were his.

The next morning we were to go to Ruda. Every detail of the trip was discussed at length—which horses, which vehicles, which road—and finally I got into the break with Henia. Since Frederick could not make up his own mind we tossed for it and I turned out to be her companion. The morning shimmered into the distance, the lane wound

over the hilly ground, deep paths with yellow walls ran
into it, here and there a bush, a tree, a cow, ahead of us
jogged the carriage with Karol driving. She—wearing a
Sunday dress, a coat white with dust over her shoulders—
a fiancée going to join her fiancé. So, no longer able to
restrain myself, I said, after a few introductory remarks:
"Congratulations! You'll soon be married, with a family.
You'll have children!"

She replied: "Yes, I'll have children."

She had replied, but how! Obedient, zealous, like a
schoolgirl. Reciting her lesson. Transformed into an obedient child at the thought of her own children. We drove
along at a good pace. . . We could see the tails and the fat
cruppers of the horses move rhythmically. Yes! She wanted
to marry the lawyer! She wanted children from him! And
she had the audacity to say it while the figure of her young
lover could be seen silhouetted in the distance.

We passed a heap of rubbish thrown on the side of the
road, and soon after, two acacias.

"Do you like Karol?"

"Of course. . . we've known each other. . ."

"Since you were children, I know. But I'm asking if you
feel anything else for him?"

"Me? I like him very much."

"Very much? Is that all? Then why did you crush that
worm together?"

"Which worm?"

"And his trousers? The trousers you turned up by the
shed?"

"Which trousers? Oh yes, of course, they were too long.
What about it?"

How blinding was this smooth wall of lies, constructed
in good faith, of lies which she did not think were lies! But
how could I force her to tell the truth? This being sitting

next to me, frail, indistinct, and vague, who was not a woman, but was only the embryo of a woman, this provisional entity who only existed so as not to be herself, who was killing herself.

"Karol's in love with you!"

"Him? He's not in love with me or with anyone else. . . all he wants to do is. . . well, to go to bed with somebody. . . " And then she added something which obviously gave her pleasure. "He's just a kid, and what's more. . . well, it's better not to mention it!"

It was clearly an allusion to Karol's rather confused past, but in spite of everything I thought I could detect a certain affection in these words, a shade of "organic" attraction, possibly due to their friendship. At any rate, it was not said reproachfully, but rather as though she liked the idea of it, with a note of familiarity in her voice. As Albert's fiancée she obviously felt that she had to condemn Karol, and yet she seemed to cling to him in the tempestuous destiny common to their generation, born in the shadow of the war. I immediately hung on to this concept, trying to exploit this familiar tone. I told her casually, chummily, that she was no saint and could surely go to bed with him, couldn't she? She took it very well, far better than I had expected, even with a certain eagerness or a strange docility. She immediately agreed with me that "she could, of course," particularly since she had done it once before, last year, with a chap from the A.K. who had hidden in their house. "You won't tell my parents, will you?" Why was she letting me into her secrets so easily? Immediately after her engagement to Albert, too? I asked if her parents suspected anything (about the chap from the A.K.), to which she replied: "They certainly suspect something because they caught us at it. But in actual fact they don't suspect anything."

"In actual fact"—what a brilliant expression! One could say everything, mean everything with it. A magical expression which concealed everything. We were now descending on Brzustowa, across a row of lime trees—the shadows speckled with sunlight, the horses slowing down, the harnesses falling around their necks, the sand squeaking under the wheels. . .

"All right! That's what I mean! Why not? There was the chap from the A.K. What's wrong with this one?"

"No."

The ease with which women say "no!" This capacity for refusing! This "no" which is always at hand—and once they find it in themselves they are pitiless. But. . . could she be in love with Albert? Was this the reason for her continence? I suggested that it would be quite a blow for Albert if he were to find out about her "past"—for him who respected her so deeply, who had such high principles and was so religious. I expressed the hope that she should never tell him about it, no, she really should not put him to that test. . . him who believed so firmly in their spiritual harmony. . . She interrupted me, deeply offended: "But what are you talking about? Don't you think I've got any morals?"

˒ "He's got Catholic morals."

"So have I. I am a Catholic."

"What? Do you go to Communion?"

"Of course."

"Do you believe in God? Literally, like a Catholic?"

"If I didn't believe in God I wouldn't go to confession and Communion. What did you think? Albert's morals suit me very well. And his mother is almost like my mother. You'll see what sort of a woman she is! For me it's an honor to marry into a family like that." And, after a moment's silence, she added, pulling lightly on the reins: "At any rate, if I marry him I won't be sleeping around with everybody."

The sand. The lane. Going uphill.

The vulgarity of her last words—why? "I won't be sleeping around with everybody." She could have put it more delicately. But it was an ambiguous sentence. She expressed her desire for purity and dignity in an undignified, degrading way, in an exciting way, exciting for me, because that made her closer to Karol. And again, as on the day before with Karol, I felt a pang of resentment: it was really impossible to find out anything from them because whatever they felt, said, and thought was only a game to excite each other, to provoke and seduce each other, a narcissistic orgy —and they were the first to suffer from their seduction. This girl?. . . this girl who was nothing but an attraction for herself, a desire to please, molded with coquetry, malleable, flexible, and enchanting—sitting next to me, in her little coat, with her little, far too little, hands. "If I marry him I won't be sleeping around with everybody." This sounded strict, she was regaining control for Albert's sake, through Albert—but it was also a familiar, seductive admission of her own weakness. Even when she was being virtuous she was devilishly exciting. . . but in the distance, going up a slope, was the carriage with Karol driving. . . Karol. . . Karol. . . Driving. Going up a slope. In the distance. Was it because he appeared "in the distance" or "going up a slope?". . . this sudden apparition, this irruption of Karol had something supremely provocative about it, and, in a fury, pointing to him, I said:

"But you love crushing worms with him, don't you?"

"What are you going on about the worm for? He crushed it and I finished it off, that's all."

"You saw how much the beast was suffering!"

"What are you getting at?"

Once again I was foxed. She was sitting next to me. For a moment I thought of giving up, of retreating. . . My position, this way of reveling in their eroticism—no, it could not last! I ought to find some other occupation, something more suitable, more serious! Was it so hard to return to my normal condition, where other problems absorbed my attention and where I tended to despise these little games with the young? But when we are excited we begin to adore our excitement, it excites us and we lose interest in everything else! Pointing once again at Karol with my compromising finger I said insistently, hoping to corner her and extort a confession:

"You're not yours. You're someone else's. And this someone is him. You're his!"

"Me? His? You're crazy!"

She roared with laughter. Their continual, incessant laughter—his and hers—laughter which obscured everything. It made one despair!

She rejected him. . . laughing. . . She rejected him with a laugh. Her laugh was short, and stopped abruptly, it was only the hint of a real laugh—but in this brief instant I saw his laugh in her laugh. The same smiling mouth with beautiful, white teeth. It was "pretty". . . alas, alas! it was "pretty." They were both "pretty." That was why she did not want to!

7

Ruda. We stepped out of the two vehicles before the front door. Albert appeared and ran up to his fiancée to greet her on the threshold—and greeted us with that quiet courtesy which distinguished him. In the hall we kissed the hand of a withered little old lady who smelled of herbs and medicine, and who delicately squeezed our fingers. The house was full, the day before some relatives from near Lwow had arrived unexpectedly. They had been put up on the first floor, but there were beds even in the drawing room; maidservants were hard at work, children were playing on the floor amid bundles and empty suitcases. We therefore decided to go back to Poworna for the night—but Albert's mother, Amelia, protested violently: "You can't do that!" she said. "You'll all be able to fit in somehow." There were other reasons, too, for returning to Poworna. Under a vow of secrecy Albert told us men that there were two fellows from the A.K. spending the night in the house and, according to them, there was going to be some sort of action in the area. All this made the atmosphere rather tense. We sat in the armchairs in the large drawing room, dark in spite of the many windows, and the old lady turned politely to Frederick and me, and asked us about our life in Warsaw. Her incredibly old and withered head hung over her neck like a star; she was undoubtedly a remarkable

woman and the air we breathed in this house had a quality
of its own. No, it would be impossible to speak too highly
of her: we were not dealing with one of those church mice
only too common in the provinces, but with an extraordinary personality. It is hard to say how that became apparent. A respect for the human being, not unlike Albert's,
but still deeper. A courtesy founded on the subtlest of
feelings. An almost inspired tactfulness, imbued with
spirituality, and at the same time of incredible simplicity.
Immense integrity. Finally the impression of a rigorous,
categorical force, of a superior reason dominating the house,
of absolute reason, demolishing all doubts. For us, for
me and undoubtedly also for Frederick, this highly spiritual
house suddenly became a wonderful place of rest, an oasis.
A metaphysical principle reigned here, a transcendental
principle, in short, the Catholic God, liberated from all
corporal bonds, and far too dignified to go chasing after
Karol and Henia with us. It was as though the hand of this
intelligent mother had given us a slap calling us to order
and everything returned to normal instantaneously. Henia
with Karol, Henia plus Karol, returned to what they were,
to their perfectly normal youth—and Henia with Albert
became more important, but only because of their future
marriage and their love. But we, we the adults, recovered
the sense of our maturity, and we suddenly found ourselves
so firmly and so eternally immersed in it that there could
no longer be a question of any threat coming from them,
from below. In short, we had regained the "lucidity"
which Albert had already brought us at Poworna, but
not as forcibly as today. The weight of their young knees
on our chests became less oppressive.

Frederick came to life. Released from their damnable
young feet he believed again in himself—and he breathed
again—and he reappeared in his former glory. What he

said was by no means dazzling, just ordinary sentences
designed to sustain the conversation, but the smallest detail became important when he loaded it with his personality, his emotion, and his lucidity. Even the most commonplace word, "the window," for example, or "the bread," or
"thank you" had an entirely different flavor on these lips
which knew so well what they were saying. He said casually
"one enjoys the little comforts of life," and this immediately became important, if only as an admission of the importance he attached to it. His own particular style, his way
of existing became perceptible, was suddenly present in its
concrete form. If man could only be judged by the importance he attaches to himself we were confronted by a
giant, because he apparently represented an extraordinary
phenomenon to himself. Extraordinary not on the scale of
social values but as a being, as an existence. And this
solitary grandeur was welcomed by Albert and his mother
as though the respect they could show for somebody constituted one of their subtlest pleasures. Even Henia, des-
tined to play the leading part in this household, slipped
into the background, and there was soon only Frederick.

"Come with me," said Amelia. "I shall show you the
view from the terrace before we go in to lunch."

She was so absorbed by him that she spoke to him alone,
totally ignoring Henia, her parents, and me. . . We accompanied them to the terrace from where the ground could
be seen stretching in gentle hillocks down to the flat, almost invisible surface of the river, which lay there like a
corpse. It was pretty. But Frederick blurted out:

"The barrel."

And he was confused. . . because instead of admiring
the landscape he had noticed something as insignificant and
uninteresting as a barrel lying under a tree. He did not

know how he could have said that, or how to extricate himself. And Amelia repeated, like an echo:

"The barrel."

She said it in a whisper, but penetratingly, as though she were confirming what he had said, in total agreement with him—as though she too were used to those fortuitous initiations into a fortuitous object which extracts all its importance from the very importance you attach to it. . . ah, yes, indeed, they both had much in common! We sat down to lunch with the entire family of refugees and their children—but all these guests, this crowd, these children running about, the improvised meal, were most unpleasant. The meal was exhausting. And the "situation" was constantly being discussed, the general one in connection with the German retreat, and the local one; I lost my way in the rustic tone of the conversation, so different from those we had in Warsaw, I did not understand half of what they were saying but I asked no questions, I did not want to ask any, what was the point of it? In all events I would soon understand. Sitting in this din I drank, and all I saw was that Amelia, who supervised the meal from the heights of her withered little head, continued to treat Frederick with special attention, with special concentration, even rather nervously—she looked in love with him. Love? It was more the inexhaustible magic of Frederick's curious lucidity, a magic I had so frequently been aware of myself. He was so penetratingly, irrevocably conscious. Amelia, whose mind must have been stimulated by meditation and spiritual exercises, had immediately sensed the value of her partner. Somebody with immense powers of concentration, never allowing himself to be deceived or distracted from the essence of things, somebody serious to the ultimate degree, who made everyone else seem childish. Having discovered Frederick she wanted to know how this man was going to accept her: whether the truth she had for so long cultivated within herself would meet with approval or refusal.

She realized he was not a believer; that was evident from the precautions she took, from the way she kept her distance. She knew there was an abyss between them and yet it was from him that she wanted recognition and confirmation. All the people she had hitherto known had been believers but they had never delved deep enough—this man however, an unbeliever, was unfathomably deep, and could therefore not fail to recognize her depth, he was an "extremist" and must understand her "extremism"—because he "knew," he "understood," he "felt." Amelia wanted to confront his extremism with hers; I suppose she was like a provincial artist who manages, for the first time in his life, to show his work to a real connoisseur—but her work was herself, it was her life she wanted him to do justice to. She was not of course able to express this, and would probably have been unable to do so even if Frederick's atheism had not restrained her. And yet the sole presence of this alien depth next to her stimulated her to her very depths, and she tried to tell him, to give him to understand through her composure and inner tension, how dependent she was on him and what she expected from him.

As for Frederick, his behavior was, as usual, exquisitely tactful. And yet his contemptibility, the same he had displayed when he was raking the path, when he admitted defeat, gradually began to appear under Amelia's influence. It was the contemptibility of impotence. It was all reminiscent of copulation, spiritual copulation, of course. Amelia wanted him to recognize if not her God, at least her faith, but this man was not capable of such a moral standard, condemned as he was to submit to the eternal terror of the man who exists, a cold mind which nothing could warm—he was as he was—and he simply observed Amelia

to ascertain whether she was as she was. This, in the heat
of her fervor, seemed lethally impotent. Frederick's atheism
increased when confronted by Amelia's victorious theism,
the contradiction between them was irreparable and fatal.
What was more, under the influence of this extreme spirituality, he affirmed himself physically and I saw his hand,
for example, become very, very much a hand, more and
more a hand (I do not know why that reminded me of the
worm). I also noticed the look with which he undressed
her like a Don Juan with a little girl, a look which betrayed
the question: what does she look like naked? Not out of any
erotic desire, of course, but simply to have a better idea of
whom he was talking to. Under this look she wilted and
suddenly fell silent—she had just realized that for him
she was only what he saw, nothing more.

This took place on the terrace, after lunch. She got up
and turned to Frederick:

"May I lean on your arm? Let's go for a walk in the
garden."

She took his arm. Maybe, with this physical contact, she
wanted to tame him and conquer his "materiality"! They
went before us, leaning against one another like a couple of
lovers, the six of us following, like a wedding train—it
looked like an idyll; was that not how we had escorted
Henia and Albert not so long ago?

An idyll, but a tragic one. I presume Amelia experienced
a cold shudder as she intercepted the look that undressed
her—because nobody had ever treated her like that before,
the people who surrounded her had shown nothing but
respect and love for her, ever since she was a child. What
did he know and what was the nature of his knowledge,
that he should dare treat her like that? She was absolutely
positive that the value of her spiritual effort, which had
earned her the sympathy and respect of everybody, could

not be questioned, so she did not fear for herself, she feared for the world—because another concept of the world was being opposed to hers, a concept which was no less serious, also stemming from a similar withdrawal to extreme positions.

These two serious people walked along arm in arm, over the broad meadows; the sun was already setting and was becoming red and swollen; behind us sprang shadows, growing longer and longer. Henia was walking next to Albert. Hippolytus was escorting his wife. I was on my own. And Karol. That couple in front of us deep in conversation. An insignificant conversation. They were talking about. . . Venice.

At a certain moment she stopped:

"Look around you. Isn't it beautiful?"

He replied:

"Yes, it is. Very beautiful."

He just said that to confirm it for her.

She gave a start of impatience. This reply was nonexistent, it simply evaded the real one, although it was said politely and even with a certain emotion, but the emotion of an actor. She, on the other hand, wanted him sincerely to admire this sunset, this work of God, she wanted him to honor the Creator, at least in His works. Her purity transpired from this demand.

"But please look properly. Tell me truthfully. Isn't it beautiful?"

This time, called to order, he pulled himself together, made a genuine effort to sound moved and said, as sincerely as he could:

"But I do think it's very beautiful, I think it's marvelous."

She cannot have expected any more. It was obvious that he was making an effort: as soon as he said something one

felt he was saying it so as not to say something else. . .
What could be done? Amelia decided to put her cards on
the table and said, without any transition:

"You're an atheist?"

Before committing himself to such a deliberate problem
he glanced right and left, as though he wanted to examine
the world. He said, because he had to, because he had nothing else to say, because the reply was already contained in
the question:

"I'm an atheist."

But again, he said that so as not to say something else!
That could be felt. She did not speak, every possibility of
polemic was destroyed. Had he been a real unbeliever she
could have struggled with him, she could have given her
reasons, she could have shown him the depths of her
"extremism," in short, she could have had an equal fight.
But his words only served to hide something else. What?
What? If he were neither a believer nor an unbeliever,
what was he? An abyss of murky darkness opened before
her as she was confronted by this strange "otherness," she
lost her balance, dizzy and dumfounded.

She turned back toward the house, and we followed
her, projecting on the meadows our immense shadows
which reached the distant and unknown border of the field
of stubble. A marvelously limpid evening. Amelia, I could
have sworn, began to be really frightened. She hurried
along, taking no notice of Frederick who paced along beside her—like a faithful dog. She was dumfounded and
disarmed. . . It was no longer her faith that was being attacked, she did not need to defend it—but it was her God
who was becoming useless, confronted by this atheism
which was only a mask, and she felt all alone, without a
God, left to herself, before this elusive existence, based on
an unknown principle. And the fact that this existence

should elude her compromised her irremediably. Because that proved that at every turn Catholic spirituality ran the risk of colliding with something unknown, incomprehensible, uncontrollable. She suddenly felt apprehended by someone in an entirely unknown way—and appeared to herself, in Frederick, as somebody quite incomprehensible.

On this meadow, in the twilight, our wedding train twisted like a snake. A little behind us, at an angle to our left, walked Henia and Albert, both very well behaved and civilized, well anchored in their families, he—the son of his mother, she—the daughter of her parents; and the lawyer's body felt more at ease next to this sixteen-year-old girl, surrounded by two mothers and a father. Karol was on his own, on one side, his hands in his pockets, looking bored, or maybe not; he idly moved his feet on the grass, the left one, then the right one, then the left one, then the right one, then the left one, then the right one, then the left one, in the somnolence of the green meadows, under the setting sun which still gave out some heat in spite of the cool breeze—he moved his feet, this one, that one, slowing down or hurrying up, until he was level with Frederick (who was next to Amelia). They walked a little way in silence. Karol said:

"Would you give me an old jacket?"

"What for?"

"I need one. . . To sell."

"What's that got to do with me?"

"I need one."

"Well, buy one, then!" said Frederick.

"I haven't got any dough."

"Nor have I."

"Would you give me the jacket?"

Amelia walked faster—so did Frederick—so did Karol.

"Would you give me the jacket?"

"Would you give him the jacket?"

It was Henia. She had left Albert a few yards behind. She was walking next to Karol, talking and moving just like him.

"Would you give him the jacket?"

"Would you give me the jacket?"

Frederick stopped, raised his arms comically: "Leave me in peace, children!" Amelia walked faster and faster, without turning around, so she looked as though she were being pursued by them. Why indeed did she not turn around, once at least? That was a mistake: she now looked as though she were escaping from their adolescent pranks (while her son remained in the background). But who was she escaping from, the two children, or him, Frederick? Or from him with them? Had she sensed the ambiguity of the relationship between the two adolescents? It was unlikely, she cannot have had a nose for that kind of thing and these two did not count in her eyes—Henia only mattered because she was to be Albert's future wife, but Henia and Karol—they were children, they were young. If she was escaping, then, it was from Frederick, from the familiarity with which Karol was treating him—incomprehensible to her—which had grown up here, before her eyes, which was aimed at her. . . because, under the boy's attack, this man lost the seriousness he had acquired before her. . . And this shocking familiarity had just been reinforced by the voice of her son's bride! Amelia's flight was an admission— she had seen all that, she had registered it!

The minute she moved away the two adolescents stopped pestering Frederick. Because she had moved away? Or because they had exhausted their jokes? I need not add that although Frederick was shattered by this youthful assault and looked exactly like somebody who had just escaped a gang of toughs in a suburb at night, he took every precaution to keep up appearances and to let sleeping dogs lie. Without losing any time he joined Hippolytus and Maria and tried to drown these incongruities in a surge of words. What was more, he called Albert and engaged him in a banal but voluble conversation. All evening he remained as quiet as a mouse and did not even so much as glance at Henia and Karol, at Henia with Karol, and made every effort to restore calm and tranquillity. He obviously feared the awakening of the depths that Amelia had tried to provoke in him. He feared the dangerous combination with the superficiality and the youthful lightness of the adolescents, feeling that these two orders could not coexist, and he was afraid of an explosion, of the irruption of. . . Of what? Yes, yes, he was afraid of this explosive mixture of A (Amelia) multiplied by (H plus K). So, ears back, tail between his legs, and silence, hush! And he carried his zeal so far that at dinner (with the family, since the refugees from Lwow were being served in their rooms) he did not hesitate to raise his glass to the health of the betrothed, wishing them his heartfelt congratulations. He could not have behaved better. Unfortunately this strange mechanism was at work once again and made him sink deeper and deeper whenever he tried to retreat—but in this case it happened more violently, more dramatically than ever. Already the fact that he should have stood up, that he should have emerged among us, gave us a thrill of expectation and Hippolytus' wife could not suppress a nervous exclamation—because nobody knew what he was going to say, what he could say. The first words put our minds at rest, conventional and even witty as they were: waving his napkin he thanked the young couple for having illuminated his sad bachelorhood with the glow of their touching engagement, and, in a few well-turned sentences, he paid them a sympathetic tribute. . . It was only gradually, as his speech continued, that what he was not saying began to appear through what he was saying; yes, the same old thing! . . . And soon, to the horror of the orator himself, it appeared that his speech was nothing but an effort to distract our attention from the real speech, the speech without words, beyond words and full of a meaning that words could not convey. Through the well-phrased commonplaces transpired the very essence of this being; nothing could efface this face, these eyes expressing something implacable —and he, feeling he was becoming atrocious, and therefore dangerous to himself, did everything he could to seem kind and inoffensive, and embarked on a conciliating, supernatural, arch-Catholic speech about "the family as a social entity," "the national heritage," and so on. At the same time his disillusioned, implacably present face was a real insult to Amelia and her guests. The destructive force of his speech was inconceivable, and you could see this force, this marginal force, carry away the orator like a bolting horse.

He ended with a felicitation, something like:

"Ladies and gentlemen, they deserve to be happy so they will be happy!"

Which meant:

"I'm talking for the sake of talking."

Amelia thanked him eagerly:

"Thank you, thank you, we are very touched."

The sound of clinking glasses dispelled the anguish. Amelia concentrated on her duties as hostess: "Have some more meat, or some more vodka, perhaps. . . " Everyone started speaking to hear the sound of his own voice, and the din finally erased the feeling of embarrassment. The dessert, a cheesecake, was served. Toward the end of the meal Amelia got up and went into the pantry. But we, stimulated by the alcohol, joked and described to Henia the engagement feasts of the prewar days, when the tables groaned under the weight of the most delicious dishes. Karol roared with laughter and drank. I noticed that when she returned from the pantry Amelia sat down with a curious stiffness—first she stood by her chair, and then she sat down almost mechanically—but before I had time to think twice about it she fell to the ground. Everybody rushed over to her. We saw a red patch on the floor. From the kitchen came a scream, a shot rang out in the courtyard, and someone, I think it was Hippolytus, threw his jacket over the lamp. We were plunged in darkness. There was another shot. The doors were bolted and barred, Amelia was carried to a sofa, amid feverish activity in the dark. . . The jacket on the lamp caught fire, so it had to be stamped out, then there was silence and we stood, listening. Albert slipped a gun into my hands and pushed me over to the drawing room window, whispering: "Keep a lookout!" I could see the calm, silent night and the full moon, and a partly withered leaf on a branch near the window, revealing its silver belly. I gripped my gun and peered out, watching the slightest movement down there, in the shadows of the damp tree trunks. But only a sparrow moved in the scrub. Finally a door slammed, I heard someone raise his voice and other voices joined in—and I realized the moment of panic was over.

Hippolytus' wife appeared next to me: "Do you know anything about medicine? Come along. She's dying. She's been stabbed. . . Do you know anything about medicine?"

Amelia was lying on the sofa, her head on some cushions, and the dining room was full—of the refugees from Lwow, of the servants. . . their immobility maddened me, they exuded impotence. . . the same impotence that sometimes appeared on Frederick's face. . . They all seemed to have withdrawn from her, leaving her to die alone. They just

looked on. Her profile stood out, immobile, like a rock out
of the sea. Albert, Frederick, Hippolytus stood around
her. . . Would she take long to die? On the floor was a bowl
full of cotton wool and blood. But Amelia's body was not
the only one lying in the room—over there, on the floor,
in a corner, there was another one. . . I did not know what
it was or how it had got there, I could not even distinguish
it. . . I just had the impression there was something erotic
about it. . . that an erotic element had intervened. . . Karol?
Where was Karol? Leaning against a chair, he was there,
with all the rest of them, while Henia knelt down and
rested her elbows on an armchair. We were all staring at
Amelia, so fixedly that I could not detach my eyes from her
to take a more leisurely look at the other body, superfluous
and unexpected, lying in the corner of the room. Nobody
moved. But everybody gazed at her attentively and seemed
to wonder how she was going to die—because one had the
right to expect her to die an extraordinary death, and that
was what her son, Hippolytus and his wife, Henia, and even
Frederick, who did not take his eyes off her, expected.
What a paradox! They demanded something from the only
person who was incapable of moving, frozen in impotence,
and yet the only one who could act. She knew it. Suddenly
Maria ran out of the room and returned with a crucifix—it
was as though she had given the dying woman the signal
to act, and the burden of expectation fell from our hearts—
we now knew it would begin at any moment. Hippolytus'
wife, holding the cross, stood at the foot of the sofa.

Then something so scandalous happened, despite the
extreme subtlety of it, that we all had a shock. . . The dying
woman hardly glanced at the cross, turned her eyes to Frederick and would not take them off him—that was what was
so incredible! Who could have thought that she would have
shown such indifference to the crucifix, now ridiculously

useless in Maria's hands?—and this very indifference gave all
its weight to Amelia's gaze, riveted on Frederick's eyes. She
would not let him out of her sight. The unfortunate Frederick, transfixed by this dying and therefore dangerous look,
stood there turning pale, and drew himself up to attention.
They gazed at each other. Hippolytus' wife went on brandishing the crucifix but the minutes passed and it remained
out of use—a wretched, unemployed crucifix. For this saint
on her deathbed had Frederick really become more important than Christ? Was she really in love with him? No,
it was not love, it was something far more personal, this
woman saw him as her judge—she could not consent to die
before earning his approval, before proving to him that she
was as much of an "extremist" as he was, as fundamental a
phenomenon, as important. So important was his opinion
to her. That she should implore recognition and confirmation of her existence not from Christ, but from him, a
simple mortal, only provided with an exceptional consciousness, was an astonishing heresy for her, a renunciation of
the absolute in favor of life, an admission according to
which it was not God but man who had to judge other men.
At the time I obviously did not see this all so clearly, and
yet I shuddered at the sight of her gaze riveted on the eyes
of a human being, while God passed unnoticed in the hands
of Maria.

Her mortal agony, which did not actually progress under
the weight of our concentration and expectation, became
increasingly tense—we loaded it with all the tension we had
in ourselves. And I knew Frederick well enough to fear that
when confronted by such a special event, such an unusual
event as a human death, he might do something incongruous. But he went on standing at attention, as stiffly as if he
were in church, and behaved impeccably, except for his
eyes which occasionally and uncontrollably slipped from

Amelia's and peered into the room where the other body lay, still mysterious to me since I could not see it properly from where I stood; the increasingly frequent incursions of Frederick's eyes finally made me decide to look for myself. . . I went into the corner. What was my horror, or my emotion, when I saw (a boy), whose slimness was a repetition of (Karol's) slimness, and who lay there alive, and, what was more, was the incarnation of golden, fair-haired beauty, with huge black eyes and dark skin which increased the savagery of his arms and bare feet splayed on the floor!

A savage, feline, fair-haired child, of rustic beauty—a sumptuous idol, covered in dirt, who let his charms gambol on the floor. This body? This body? What was it doing? How had it got there? It was. . . it was a repetition of Karol, but an octave lower. . . and suddenly the youth in the room not only increased in number (because a couple is quite different from three) but also in quality, it was changing, becoming more savage, more base. And at once, as though by repercussion, Karol's body came to life, strengthened and amplified, and Henia, although she was kneeling piously, rushed in all her whiteness into a mysterious and guilty conspiracy with the two of them. At the same time Amelia's agony was tarnished, became suspect—what bond could there be between her and this (boy), what did he want here, at the hour of her death? I realized that the circumstances of this death were proving very ambiguous, far more ambiguous than they seemed at first sight.

Frederick, who had unconsciously put his hands in his pockets, took them out at once and pressed them to the seams of his trousers.

Albert was on his knees.

Maria was brandishing her cross because there was nothing else she could do—to put it down was quite impossible.

Amelia's finger moved, rose and began to beckon. . . to

beckon to Frederick who approached slowly. She continued to beckon until he had lowered his head to her lips, and when he had done that she said, surprisingly loudly:

"Don't go away. You'll see. I want you to see. Everything. To the end."

Frederick bowed and stepped back.

It was only then that she turned to the cross and started to pray, judging from the imperceptible tremor of her lips—finally everything returned to order: the cross, her prayer, our composure—that lasted a very long time, and the passage of time alone gauged the fervor of this prayer which nothing seemed to distract from the cross. This immobile concentration, which was nearly dead already and yet still vibrated from the sheer length of its duration, sanctified the dying woman. Albert, Hippolytus and his wife, Henia, the servants, accompanied it on their knees. Frederick knelt down too. But in vain. Because although the dying woman was totally absorbed in the crucifix, her demand remained just as powerful: she wanted him to see everything, to the end. Why? Did she want to make a final effort to convert him? Did she want to set the example of a Catholic death? Whatever happened, Frederick, not Christ, was the last resort; if she prayed to Christ it was for Frederick and it was in vain that he fell to his knees—he remained, he, not Christ, the supreme arbiter and God, because she was dying for him. What an embarrassing situation—it did not surprise me to see him hide his face in his hands. Still more so since the minutes were passing and we knew that with every one of them her life was fading—but she prolonged her prayer, so she could stretch it as far as it would go, like a string. Again her finger moved and began to beckon, this time to her son. Albert went up to his mother, his arm around Henia. Her finger pointed at them accusingly and she said rapidly:

"Swear to me at once. Love and fidelity. Quick."

They bowed over her hands. Henia burst into tears. But she had already raised her finger and beckoned again, this time to the dark corner, to the body in the corner. . . There was a movement in the room. He was picked up—I saw he was wounded in the thigh, I believe—and he was carried to the dying woman. She moved her lips and I finally thought I would know what he was doing there, this (boy), dripping with blood, what there was between them. But she suddenly gasped, once, twice, and turned white. Maria held up the crucifix. Amelia searched desperately for Frederick and, gazing at him, she died.

PART TWO

8

Frederick, who had knelt down, rose to his feet and walked into the middle of the room: "Pay your respects to her!" he shouted. "Do homage to her!" He took a bunch of roses out of a vase and cast it by the sofa, then he gave Albert his hand: "A soul worthy of the celestial throng! All we can do is to bow down humbly before her!" These words would have sounded false on the lips of any other of us, not to mention the theatrical gestures that accompanied them, but he pierced us with them as imperiously as a monarch to whom pathos is permitted—who has introduced a new naturalness, far above the norm. A monarch, a master of ceremonies! Albert, carried away by the sovereignty of this pathos, got up and squeezed his hand warmly. It looked as though this intervention of Frederick's were intended to efface the incongruities which had troubled Amelia's death, to restore it to its full glory. He walked a few steps to the right, a few steps to the left—it was as though he were writhing convulsively among us—and went up to the (boy) lying on the floor. "On your knees!" he commanded. "On your knees!" In a way this order was the logical continuation of the preceding order, but on the other hand it was clumsy, because it was given to someone who was wounded and could not move; and it seemed even clumsier when Albert, Hippolytus, and Karol, terrorized by Frederick's authority, rushed up to the (boy) to force him to his knees. Yes, it was too much! And when Karol's hands gripped the (boy) by the shoulders, Frederick flinched, fell silent, and faded away.

I was dazed, exhausted. . . so many emotions. . . and yet I knew him. . . and I knew he had just invented a new game with himself and us. . . ; in the tension created by the presence of the corpse some action was being organized in pursuit of an end known only to his imagination. It was all intentional, although the intention may not have been clear, even to himself. It was undoubtedly better to say that he only knew the beginning of the intention. Did it have anything to do with paying homage to Amelia? No, what he wanted to do was to introduce this wounded (boy), however corrosive and compromising he might be, to make him "stand out," to bring him into the open and "bind" him to Henia and Karol. But what sort of a bond could there be between them? Of course this golden savagery was well suited to our couple, if only on account of age (he too must have been about sixteen), but apart from that I did not see what they could have in common and I do not think Frederick could see it either—but he acted blindly, moved by the same obscure feeling I had, that the wounded (boy) affirmed them as a couple—"demonized" them in some way. And that was why Frederick was trying to pave the path for him to Henia and Karol.

It was only on the next day (which was entirely devoted to the preparations for the funeral) that I was given a detailed account of this fatal accident—which was moreover highly confused, strange, and almost unlikely. To reconstruct the events of the day before was not easy, and there were some desperate gaps made even worse by the fact that the only witnesses, this Olek himself, Olek Skuziak, and the old maid Valerie, were constantly going astray in the confusion of their boorish and ignorant thoughts. At any rate, it appeared that when Amelia was in the pantry she heard a noise on the kitchen stairs and had come across Olek who had slipped into the house hoping to pinch something. Hearing her coming Olek made for the first door he saw and burst into the maid's room, waking up Valerie who immediately lit a match. The rest of the story had been pieced together from her garbled account: "When I'd lit my match and seen there was someone there I had a sort of cramp in my back, so I couldn't move and the match burnt my finger—my finger's still all swollen. Then I saw Madam opposite him over by the door and she didn't move either. My match went out. One couldn't see a thing and the blinds were drawn. So I lay there and looked and I couldn't see a thing—it was pitch-black; if only the floor had creaked, but it didn't, nothing, nothing, as though there wasn't a soul! I held my breath and said a prayer, but nothing happened, it was all quiet, so I looked for the match on the floor which hadn't finished burning, but it didn't light up a thing—it just went out. Not a thing. . . if only one of them had breathed, but they didn't. . . not a thing. And then, all of a sudden. . . " (she choked as though she had swallowed a potato) "all of a sudden. . . I don't know how. . . Madam went for him! I swear it's true! She went for him! Yes, she went for his legs. . . And then they started rolling on the ground! I can't think how—God protect me —but they didn't say a word. I wanted to help, but I felt quite dizzy, then I heard a knife going into some flesh, once, twice, and then I heard it again, then they both made off and I didn't see them any more! And then I passed out proper! I passed out proper, I did!"

"But that's impossible!" said Albert. "It can't have been like that! I'll never believe my mother could. . . behave like that! This old fool's mixed everything up in her thick skull, oh, I'd rather hear a hen clucking," he shouted, "I'd rather hear a hen clucking!"

He mopped his brow.

But little Skuziak's account tallied with the maid's: Madam had gone for him, had gone for his legs and pulled him down. Holding a knife. And he not only showed wounds on his side and thigh, but also tooth marks on his neck and hands. "She bit me," he said. "I tugged her knife away, and then she fell on it. I dashed out, but the bailiff shot at me, I tumbled down and that's how they caught me."

That Amelia could have "fallen" on the knife, as he said, nobody was prepared to believe. "A lie!" said Frederick. "And as for the bites—well, for Heaven's sake, when one's fighting for one's life in a clinch with an armed bandit (because he was the one with the knife, not her). . . well, nerves and all that. . . It's not surprising. You know what instinct is, self-preservation instinct. . . " So said Frederick. Nevertheless it was odd, to say the least. . . and shocking. Amelia biting that. . . As for the knife, the whole matter was pretty obscure, because it turned out to be Valerie's knife, a long, sharp kitchen knife she used for cutting bread. The knife had been on the bed table, right next to where Amelia had stood. So it looked as though Amelia had groped for the knife and rushed at. . .

Amelia's murderer had bare feet with black soles; two fairly vulgar colors prevailed in him—the gold of his hair falling over his black eyes, as mournful as a pond in a deep wood. These colors stood out even more against the pure, almost noble flash of his teeth, their whiteness reminiscent of. . .

Well? Well what? Well, the fact was that Amelia, when she found herself in the dark with this (boy), in the grip of unbearably tense expectation, had not been able to con-

trol herself and. . . and. . . had groped for the knife. And
when she felt it she became violent. She had rushed at him
to kill him, and as they both fell to the ground she had
started to bite wildly. Her? This holy woman? At her age?
She who set an example, with her God and her principles,
of a life of devotion and moral rectitude? This seemed like
some fantasy concocted in the obtuse minds of the cook
and the little brat, like a savage legend to suit them, the
distortion of an obscure and mysterious reality beyond their
powers of comprehension. The dark of the maid's room was
multiplied by the dark of their imagination—and Albert,
totally bewildered by this dark, did not know what to do
next; this whole business killed his mother far more definitely than the knife, it poisoned her and disfigured her for
him. . . he did not know how he could rescue her image
from the fury her teeth had engraved on the sixteen-year-
old body, from this knife she had stabbed him with. Such
a death tore his life to shreds. Frederick did his best to en-
courage him: "You can't rely on what they say," he said.
"To begin with they couldn't see anything because it was
dark. And then it's so unlike your mother, it's totally out
of character; the only thing we can be sure of is that it
couldn't have happened as they said; something else must
have happened in that darkness which was as impenetrable
for them as it is for us. That's absolutely definite, there can
be no doubt about it. . . although of course. . . it all took
place in the dark. . . . " ("Well, what?" asked Albert, seeing him hesitate). . . "You know, the dark. . . the dark. . .
can be curiously uninhibiting. . . Man lives on earth, doesn't
he? Well, in the dark the earth disappears. You know, nobody's there, one's all alone. You do see that, don't you?
We're used to it, of course, we know that every time we
turn out the light it gets dark, but nevertheless there are
moments when the dark can blind us completely, you see. . .

but even in that sort of dark your mother must have stayed as she was, she can't have changed, can she? Although in this particular case the dark had something. . . " ("What?" asked Albert. "Go on!") ". . . No. Nothing. That's all nonsense. . . " ("But what?") "Nothing, really, except that this lad, this peasant lad, who's probably even illiterate. . . " ("What does it matter whether he's illiterate or not?") ". . . No, it doesn't matter, of course. . . I only mean that, in this instance, the dark was hiding youth. . . There was a barefooted child. . . it's much easier to do that to someone young. . . that is, if it had been someone more important, more serious, well. . . " ("Well what?") ". . . No, I mean it's always easier with a child, yes, easier, and in the dark, of course. . . it's easier to do that to a boy than to an adult, and. . . You're trying to make me say something I don't mean!" he shouted, and he looked really frightened, little drops of sweat stood out on his forehead. "That's just a supposition, a theory. . . Your mother would never. . . No, that's impossible, insane! Isn't it, Karol? Well, Karol?"

Why did he ask Karol? If he was afraid why did he turn on him? He was one of those people who tries to avert a disaster and only manages to precipitate it—their fear of it attracts disaster, magnifies it and creates it. As soon as he had evoked it he could not help harping on it, inciting it. If his consciousness was so dangerous it was because he associated it not with light but with darkness—for him it was an element as blind as instinct, he did not trust it, he felt he was in its control but did not know where it was taking him. And he was a bad psychologist because he was too intelligent and imaginative—in his vast vision of man there was room for everything. He could even imagine Amelia in an impossible situation. That afternoon Albert went into town "to settle" things with the police, in other words to check any stray impulse of efficiency with a substantial bribe—if the authorities were also going to start interfering God only knew where it would end. The funeral took place the next morning—a brief and obviously rushed affair. The following day we turned back to Poworna, accompanied by Albert who left the servants in charge of the house. I was not surprised—I realized he did not want to leave Henia at such a moment. The carriage went first, with the ladies, Hippolytus and Albert, and behind, the tilbury, driven by Karol, with me, Frederick, and somebody else: Olek.

We had brought him with us because we did not know what to do with him. Release him? He was a murderer. Anyhow, Albert would not have released him under any pretext, this death was far from being over, we could not leave it as it was. . . and Albert, above all, hoped he would succeed in extorting a more suitable and less shocking version of the death. So, on the floor of the tilbury, in front of the driver's seat, the adolescent murderer lay in the straw at Karol's feet, while Karol sat at an angle, his feet up on the splashboard. Frederick and I sat behind. The tilbury went uphill and downhill, following the motionless surge of the ground, the landscape opened and closed, the horses trotted along in the dust and the warm smell of corn. Frederick, sitting on the back seat, could see them both, Karol and Olek, in that combination and no other—and all four of us, in this tilbury which climbed from hill to hill, formed a strange combination, a significant composition, an odd juxtaposition. . . and the longer our silent journey lasted, the more obsessive became this figure which we formed. Karol's timidity was amazing, his frightened adolescence seemed to have lost some of its assurance under the tragic impact of the recent events and he was perfectly quiet, good, and docile. . . he was even wearing a black tie for the occasion. And yet they were both there, in front of me and

Frederick, half a yard away, on the front seat of the tilbury. The horses trotted along. Frederick, his face toward them. . . what was he trying to see? Those two adolescent figures seemed merged into one figure, so deeply were they bound by the fraternity of their age. But Karol dominated the other, holding the reins and the whip, wearing shoes, his trousers turned high up—and between them there was no sympathy or understanding, nothing but the toughness of one adolescent toward the other, this sort of brutal, hostile malevolence they felt for each other, somewhere down there, between them. And it was quite obvious that Karol belonged to us, to Frederick and me, that he was with us, people of his own class, against this lower-class playmate he had to guard. We had them in front of us for hours of this sandy lane (which occasionally broadened out into a wide road before narrowing abruptly between two chalk walls), there were two of them in front of us and this had a certain effect, created something, set them in something. . . While there in the distance we could occasionally see on the summit of the hills the carriage that bore her—the bride. The carriage came into view and vanished again, but never allowed itself to be forgotten; sometimes it could not be seen for a long time but it inevitably reappeared—and the oblique squares of the fields and the strips of the meadows glided past us, and furled and unfurled around us—in all this tedious geometry, drowned in distant, fleeting perspectives, hung Frederick's face, his profile next to mine. What was he thinking about? What? We were behind the carriage, we were following the carriage; Karol, this other boy lying under his feet, with golden hair, black eyes, and dirty bare feet, seemed gradually to undergo a chemical transformation, he continued to follow the carriage as one star follows another, but he already existed with a playmate— playfully—his whole body in the grip of this mixture of himself with the other boy, united with him in such a way that it would not have surprised me suddenly to see them eating cherries or apples together. The horses trotted along. Yes, that must have been what Frederick thought about them—or did he imagine that that was what I was thinking?—and his face was next to mine and I no longer knew in which of us these thoughts had originated. Anyhow, when we arrived in Poworna after having driven for hours and hours, these two playmates were already "together for Henia," united in connection with her under the effect of that long journey behind her and before us.

We put the prisoner in a little lumber room with a barred window. His wounds were superficial and he might have escaped. Exhausted by the long journey we fell into bed; I slept deeply all night and part of the morning, and the next morning I was assailed by imprecise impressions as irritating as a fly buzzing in one's nose. I could not catch this buzzing, elusive fly—what sort of a fly was it? Already before lunch, when I questioned Hippolytus about some detail to do with the recent events, I detected a change of tone in his reply—he was not offensive, simply a little haughty, or disdainful or proud, as though he were bored with the subject and had other fish to fry. Other fish to fry when there had just been this murder? I noticed a new inflection in Albert's voice—how can I put it?—something dry, and even slightly arrogant. Arrogant? Why arrogant? The change of tone was as subtle as it was shocking, because how could Albert give himself such airs two days after this death? My overstrained nerves made me immediately suspect that the center of atmospheric pressure had moved in our sky and that a fresh wind was blowing—but what wind? Something had changed. It seemed to be changing direction. My fears only took shape when I caught a glimpse of Hippolytus going through the dining room and saying (dropping his voice as he did so): "What a mess, I say, what a mess!" Then he suddenly sat down on a chair, morosely. . . then sprang up, harnessed the horses and drove off. Now I knew something was going on, I was positive, but I did not want to ask anybody and it was only late that afternoon, that, seeing Frederick and Albert deep in conversation, walking around the lawn, I went up to them hoping to discover the cause of this change. Nothing of the kind. They were still discussing the death of two days ago—but in the same tone as the day before—it was an intimate discussion in a whisper. Frederick, his head down, staring at his shoes, continued to dissect this death, deduced, searched, analyzed, reflected. . . until Albert, at the end of his tether, begged to be given time to breathe, even suggesting it was tactless to torment him thus! "What?" said Frederick. "What do you mean by that?" Albert begged for mercy. The events were still too recent, he had not had time to get used to it, it was so unexpected, so appalling! It was then that Frederick swooped onto his soul like an eagle.

Maybe the comparison is too emphatic. But I really did see him dive onto this soul—dive from above. There was neither compassion nor consolation in what he said, on the contrary, there was the desire to see the son drain the cup of his mother's death to the dregs. In the same way, in exactly the same way as Catholics relive Christ's passion, minute by minute. To start with he pointed out that he was not a Catholic. That he had no so-called moral principles. That he was not virtuous. "Then why, you will ask me," he said, "in whose name do I require you to drain this cup to the dregs? I shall reply that it is solely in the name of development. What is man? Who can tell? Man is a mystery." (This commonplace appeared on his lips like something disgraceful and sarcastic, like a pain. . . .) "An angelic and demonic abyss, steeper than a mirror! But we must" (this "must" was confidential and dramatic) "we must get to the heart of the matter. That's inevitable, you know. It's necessary for our development. The law is fulfilled in the history of mankind as it is in the history of every individual. Take a child. A child begins, a child is not, a child is a child, in other words an introduction, an initiation. . . And an adolescent" (he almost spat the word out) "what does he know? What can he feel. . . this embryo? But we?. . . We?" he shouted. "We?"

And he added by the way:

"I communicated with your mother deeply and instantaneously. Not because she was a Catholic. But because she submitted to an inner need for seriousness. . . you know that. . . she was not frivolous. . . "

He looked him in the eye—something he hardly ever did —and this troubled Albert deeply, but he did not dare look away.

"She always went. . . to the heart of the matter."

"What shall I do?" shouted Albert, throwing up his arms. "What shall I do?"

Had he been speaking to anyone else he would not have dared shout like that, or throw up his arms. Frederick took him by the arm and started walking, pointing forward with his other hand: "Live up to it," he said. "Do as you like. But whatever you do, do it like her, scrupulously and seriously."

Seriousness as a basic demand of maturity—no relaxation, nothing that could even momentarily attenuate the severity of his look which persisted in getting to the heart of the matter. . . Albert had no idea how to defend himself from such severity—because it was severity. Otherwise he could have doubted the seriousness of his behavior, the sincerity of this gesticulation. . . but all this performance was being acted under the severe invocation demanding him to as-

sume full consciousness; in Albert's eyes this demand was
incontestable. His Catholicism rebelled against the savagery
of atheism (for the believer the atheist is a savage) and
Frederick's world seemed to him like a chaos deprived of
its master, therefore of law, populated solely with the un-
limited arbitration of man. And yet as a Catholic he felt
he could not neglect the moral order, even if it were from
such impious and savage lips. What was more, Albert
trembled at the idea of squandering his mother's death—
he was afraid of not living up to his drama and of not
living up to his love and his respect. And still more than
Frederick's impiety he feared his own mediocrity, all that
made him an honest, "bourgeois" lawyer. So he clung to
Frederick's calm superiority, seeking a support in him. Ah,
it did not matter how, it did not matter with whom, but he
had to experience this death! Live through it! Suck it dry!
For this he needed this savage gaze which got to the heart
of the matter, he needed this strange, this fearful, relentless
drive into experience.

"But what should I do with young Skuziak?" he shouted.
"I ask you: who's to judge him? Have we got the right to
keep him prisoner? Very well, we didn't give him up to the
police, that was impossible—but we can't keep him in that
lumber room indefinitely!"

He brought the matter up next day, when Hippolytus returned, but only succeeded in extracting a shrug of the
shoulders: "That's no problem! No use getting worked up
about it! Keep him in the lumber room! Give him up to the
police! Give him a good hiding! Let him go! Do what you
like!" And when Albert tried to make him see reason by
saying that, after all, he was his mother's murderer, Hippolytus got annoyed: "Murderer? He's no murderer, he's
just a little shit! Do what you like with him, but leave me
in peace, I've got other things to do!" He simply did not

want to discuss it; he gave the impression that this whole murder only mattered to him from one side, that of Amelia's corpse—and was totally unimportant from the other, that of the murderer. And anyhow he was obviously worried about something else. Frederick, who was leaning against the large porcelain stove, suddenly moved, as though he were going to say something, but just whispered: "Aaah! . . . " He did not say it aloud. He just whispered it. And since we were not expecting the whisper it resounded in the room more forcibly than if Frederick had spoken aloud—and as he whispered he emerged in his whisper while we waited for the rest of what he had to say. He said nothing. Then Albert, who had now learned to detect the slightest change in Frederick's attitude, asked:

"What? Were you going to say something?"

Having been asked a question Frederick glanced around the room.

"Yes, I mean. . . with him, with somebody like that, you can do anything. . . absolutely anything."

"Like that?" Hippolytus burst out in inexplicable anger. "Like what?"

Frederick explained himself, slightly disconcerted:

"Like that, that's obvious, isn't it? You can do anything with him. Whatever you like. Whatever you want."

"The other day you said the same thing about my mother," said Albert suddenly. "That my mother could have. . . with the knife. . . because. . . " He began to stammer. At which Frederick replied, with evident shame:

"No, nothing. I just said it like that. . . Don't let's talk about it."

What an actor! You could see his game quite clearly, he made no attempt to conceal it. But you could also see what it cost him, you could really see him turn pale and tremble as he ended it. As far as I could make out the game consisted in trying to give this murder and this murderer as ambiguous a character as possible—but perhaps he was not trying, perhaps he was submitting to a necessity stronger than himself in his pallor and fear. It was a game, of course, but a game which created him and created the situation. Finally everybody felt slightly uneasy. Hippolytus decided to go out, Albert fell silent. But the blows dealt by the player had hit home, nevertheless, and Olek, in his lumber room, became more and more compromising and it was as though the whole atmosphere were poisoned by a strange and incomprehensible determination. (I knew whom it was aimed at and what the point of it was. . . .) Every evening Olek's wounds had to be washed and dressed, and it was Frederick who did this, since he knew a certain amount about medicine—with Karol's help. And Henia held the lamp. This procedure was as significant as it was compromising, because all three of them stood bowed around him, each one holding something to justify this posture, Frederick the cotton wool, Karol a bowl and a bottle of spirits, Henia the lamp; but this triple bow over the wounded thigh escaped in some way from the objects they were holding and became a pure, gratuitous bow. While the lamp burned. Then Albert shut himself in with him and questioned him —alternately conciliating and threatening—but the inferiority of the boy and his peasant stupidity were impenetrable; he repeated the same thing over and over again: that she had rushed at him and started biting him, and what could he do? And, as he gradually got used to the questions he became familiar with the answers.

"Madam bit as hard as she could. You can still see the marks."

When Albert returned from these interminable interrogations, as exhausted as if he had just recovered from a long illness, Henia came and sat next to him, silent and faith-

ful. . . Karol set the table, or looked through old maga-
zines. . . and when I looked at her, striving to see her "with
Karol" I could not believe my eyes, and could not recapture
that which had formerly excited me— and I denied my own
crazy imagination. There was nothing between them, absolutely nothing! She was only with Albert! But with him
she was insatiable. What an appetite! And what impetuous
desire! What violent desire! How greedily she approached
him, like a man with a little girl! I apologize, I had nothing
improper in mind, I only wanted to say that she attacked
his soul with unbridled lust: Albert's conscience, his honor,
his sense of responsibility, his respectability, and all the
sorrows attached to it, were the object of her desire, she
was so avid of his maturity that one could have sworn his
baldness was more seductive than his mustache! All this,
of course, in her peculiar passivity—she simply absorbed
his maturity, clinging to him affectionately. And she surrendered herself to the caress of this masculine hand which
was nervous, fine and adult, she was so eager for seriousness
in the face of this dramatic death (which surpassed her inexperienced precocity), trying to take hold of other people's maturity. The little wretch! Because instead of being
brilliant and beautiful, as she could have been with Karol,
she chose this lawyer and sought contact with his pampered
ugliness! The lawyer was grateful and caressed her gently.
While the lamp burned. Several days went by like this. One
afternoon Hippolytus told us he was expecting a new guest,
Mr. Siemian, who would be paying a visit. . . And he muttered, observing his fingernail: "He'll be paying us a visit."
    And he closed his eyes.
    When we heard this news we did not ask any questions.
From the morose resignation in his voice it was clear that
he was not even trying to disguise the truth. Behind this
"visit" lurked a net which involved us all, which opposed

us to each other—a conspiracy. Each of us could only say as much as he was permitted to say—the rest consisted of heavy, oppressive silence and hazardous suppositions. The dull menace that had for some days troubled the unanimity of our feelings born from the tragic events at Ruda, became more evident and the weight that had oppressed us was transported from a recent past into an immediate and dangerous future. That evening, in the rain, a fine, cutting rain of the sort that drizzles all night, a cab drew up in front of the steps and through the half-open door of the hall I saw a tall man in an overcoat, his hat in his hand, follow Hippolytus, who held a lamp, up the stairs to the first floor where a room had been prepared for him—A sudden draft blew through the open door, Hippolytus almost dropped the lamp, and the door slammed. I recognized the man. Yes, I knew him by sight, although he did not know me. . . and I suddenly felt trapped in this house. I happened to know that this man was an important figure in the Resistance, one of the leaders, with a number of daring exploits to his name, and that he was wanted by the Germans. . . There was no doubt about it, it was he and if it was he his arrival heralded the unforeseen, because we were at his mercy: his audacity was no longer his own, by exposing himself he exposed us, too, he could involve us in some murky project—if he asked us something we could not refuse. Because the nation united us, we were comrades and brothers-in-arms—a brotherhood which was as cold as ice, everyone was someone else's tool, everyone could use anyone else pitilessly, for the common cause.

This man, both so close and so dangerously alien, had passed by me like a menacing ghost, and everything was suddenly contracted and stiff in mystery. I was aware of the risk he was making us run and yet I could not control a vague feeling of disgust for all these trappings—action,

Resistance, the leader, conspiracy—like a bad novel, a late incarnation of more or less insane childhood dreams. To destroy our games I would rather have had anything, but not that, not that. The nation and its romanticism constituted for me an undrinkable potion concocted to spite and anger me. But we could not be particular and reject what fate offered us. I met "the leader" when he came down to dinner. He looked like an officer—which, indeed, he was —a cavalry officer, from the Eastern borders, the Ukraine probably, over forty, his face darkened by his close-shaven growth of beard, a thin, elegant, and charming man. He greeted us all—it was obviously not the first time he had been here—and he kissed the ladies' hands. "I know, I've heard the ghastly news! Do you come from Warsaw, gentlemen?. . ." From time to time he closed his eyes and looked like someone who had been traveling for hours by train. . . He sat at the end of the table; he was obviously supposed to be here as a technician, as an expert on cattle-breeding or seed-sowing—a precaution for the benefit of the servants. As for us, his table companions, we clearly knew who he was—and yet the conversation languished and foundered. In the meantime strange things were happening at the end of the table, with Karol. Yes, our (young) Karol, whom the visitor's presence had put into a state of military obedience and servile eagerness—was suddenly intoxicated by loyalty, on edge, toying with death—a soldier, a partisan, a conspirator, a murderous and silent force in his rough hands and brawny arms, ready to obey, awaiting the order, competent in action. And he was not the only one to change. Was it because of Karol? All this romantic mediocrity, so irritating a moment ago, dissolved miraculously and we all communicated in the feeling that force and truth lie in unity. We sat at the table like a military detachment awaiting orders, ready for action. The Resistance, combat, the enemy. . . these words were suddenly imbued with a truth more real than everyday life and burst into the room like a cool wind; impervious to the painful disparity of Henia and Karol we were all brothers-in-arms. And yet this fraternization lacked purity! In reality—this was unbearable, and, in a word, foul. Because, between ourselves, were we adults not slightly repulsive and ridiculous in this battle? as somebody too old to make love is when he makes love? Was this in character with Frederick's slimness, Hippolytus' bloated enormity, Maria's evanescence? The detachment we formed was a reservists' detachment and we were united in decay—melancholy and disgust presided over our fraternization in battle and enthusiasm. At moments it surprised me that enthusiasm and fraternization could still exist. But at other moments I wanted to shout to Henia and Karol: Go away, don't have anything to do with us! Flee from our dirt and our farce! But they (yes, she too) did not want to leave us—they clung to us, stuck to us, offered themselves to us, they were at our command, ready for anything, for our sake, with us, on a signal from the leader! This lasted the whole meal. At least I felt it did. Did I feel that, or did Frederick?

Who knows, maybe it is one of the obscurest mysteries of humanity—and one of the most complex—the mystery of such "communion" between different generations. . . how, and which way does youth suddenly become accessible to maturity and vice versa? In this case the officer held the key to the mystery, because, as an officer, he was bound to the soldier and even more to the young soldier. . . this was evident after dinner when Frederick suggested taking Siemian to the lumber room to show him the murderer. Personally I never believed this proposition to be gratuitous, I knew the presence of Olek-the-young-murderer in the lumber room was becoming more and more urgent, almost unbearable, since Karol had offered himself to the officer. We went up—Siemian, Frederick, myself, Henia, and Karol —with the lamp. In the barred room he lay on some straw —asleep—and when we stood around him he stirred and shielded his eyes with his hand. Childishly. Karol shone the lamp on him. Siemian motioned to Karol not to wake him. In him he saw Amelia's murderer, but Karol was not shining the lamp on him as a murderer but far more as a young soldier—as a comrade. As a recruit for conscription. And Henia stood behind him and watched him shine the lamp on the boy. Karol the soldier shining a lamp on another soldier for the officer, that struck me as singular and worth a great deal of attention—it was a cordial, fraternal gesture, from soldier to soldier, but a cruel one, serving him up. Even more significant was this boy shining a lamp on another boy for an adult—although I did not quite know what it signified.

In this lumber room with its barred window we witnessed a mute explosion of these three children around the lamp and in its light—and their silent explosion released something else, unknown to us, something discreet and eager. Siemian gave them a glance, which only lasted a second, but that was enough for me to realize that he was not unaware of this.

9

Have I already mentioned the four small islands, separated from each other by canals covered with green lichen, which formed the natural prolongation of the pond? Little bridges had been built over the canals. A path, at the end of the garden, wound through the clusters of hazels, syringa, and thuyas, and made it possible to skirt this marshy archipelago of stagnant water by land. As I was going along this path one day it suddenly struck me that one of these islands differed from the others. . . how?. . . why?. . . a fleeting impression, but the garden was too deeply involved in our games for me to be able to overlook it. And yet. . . no, nothing. The corpse of this island, and its few trees with their high foliage, was dead. It was tea-time on a sultry day, and the canal was almost dry, its muddy crust with scattered puddles of green water glinting in the sun, the reeds growing triumphantly on the banks. In our situation every trace of anything unusual would have to be submitted to immediate inspection. So I crossed over to the other bank. The little island inhaled the heat, the grass grew high and thick, invaded by legions of ants, while the treetops led their lofty existences in closed distinction. I made my way through the bushes and. . . Just a minute! . . . What a surprise!

There was a bench. Henia was sitting on the bench, but

her legs looked most peculiar: one of them was encased in a stocking and shoe, while the other was naked to above the knee. . . and, stranger still, he too, lying at her feet in the grass, had uncovered one leg, his trouser rolled up above the knee. Next to him, his shoe with his sock in it. She was looking away. He was not looking at her either, his head in his arm, in the grass. No, no, the whole scene would not have seemed so shocking had it not been so incompatible with their natural rhythm, so set, motionless, and alien. . . and these legs, so curiously naked, one of each pair glistening in its nakedness, in the stifling humidity, interrupted only by the splashes of the frogs! He with a naked leg and she with a naked leg! Maybe they had been paddling in the water. . . no, it was something else, the explanation was not so simple. . . he with a naked leg and she with a naked leg! Her leg stirred and stretched out. She rested her foot on his foot. Nothing else.

I looked on. I was suddenly staggered by my stupidity. Oh! How could I have been so naive—together with Frederick—to think that there was nothing between them. . . to be deceived by appearances! The denial was there, before my eyes, as brutal as a bludgeon stroke. So this was where they met, on the island. . . a long, silent scream of relief rang out—while their contact continued, without a movement, without a sound, without even a look (because they still looked away). He with a naked leg and she with a naked leg.

Very well. . . But. . . No, it was impossible. In all that there was something indubitably false, incomprehensible, perverse. . . What was the origin of this immobility, as though they had been bewitched? And this coldness in their game? For a fraction of a second I had the insane idea that *it must be like that, that it was like that and in no other way that that should take place between them*, that that was more true than if. . . Nonsense! And I immediately had another idea: this was all a show, an act! They must have known, by some miracle, that I was going to go by and they were doing it on purpose—for me. That was all for me, no doubt about it, made for my dreams, for my eyes! For me, for me, for me! Spurred on by this idea that it was for me I threw caution to the winds and left my hiding place behind the bushes. And there the picture was complete: Frederick was sitting on a heap of dried pine needles, under a pine tree. It was for him!

I stopped! . . . As he saw me he said to them:

"You'll have to do it once more."

And at that moment, although I did not understand a thing I felt frozen by the breath of their youthful shamelessness. Their depravity. They still did not move—their youthful freshness was icily cold.

Frederick came up to me, charming. "Well, how are you, my dear Witold?" (A perfectly unnecessary question since we had seen each other less than an hour ago.) "What do you think of their pantomime?" (He gestured toward them with a sweep of his arm.) "They're not bad, are they? Ha, ha, ha!" (This laugh was unnecessary too, but loud.) "Beggars can't be choosers! . . . Did you know about my partiality for stage direction? I was an actor at one point, were you aware of that little biographical detail?"

He took me by the arm and led me around the clearing, gesticulating in a wildly theatrical way. The others looked at us without a word. "I had an idea. . . for a film. . . but some scenes were a little too outspoken, they still have to be adapted and practiced on living material. That'll do for today. You can get dressed."

And without even glancing at them he led me to the bridge, discussing his ideas loudly and volubly. In his opinion the modern method of writing plays and scripts "without taking the actors into consideration" was out of date. You had to start with the actors, "combine them" in some way, and construct the play on the successive combinations. The theater was to "bring out the latent state of living men and deal with their own range of possibilities." The actor "was not to incarnate some imaginary character, to pretend to be what he was not—on the contrary, it was the character who had to be adapted to him and fit the actor like a glove." "I'm trying," he added with a smile, "to do something like this with these children, I've promised them a little present as a reward, because it's hard work! Ah, the country gets pretty boring if one isn't doing anything, one has to do something if only for reasons of health, my dear Witold, if only for reasons of health! I don't want to show off this sort of thing, of course, because—well—it might be a little too daring for Hippo and his better half, I'd rather not risk any gossip! . . ." He spoke loudly, making his voice ring out, and I, next to him, staring at the ground, could not get the flea of that discovery out of my ear, and hardly listened to what he was saying. Ah, the artful dodger! The old fox! The schemer! He made them do things, he thought up little games for them! And all that cynically and perversely! And the flame of his depravity consumed me, I could hardly control myself, at the mercy of pangs of the most sordid jealousy! And the burning reflections of imagination lit up this cold licentiousness, both innocent and diabolic, especially hers, yes, especially hers, because it was, after all, a bit much for this tender and faithful bride to go in for this kind of thing in the bushes. . . all for the promise of a "little present."

"What an interesting theatrical experiment," I replied. "Most interesting! You've got something there!" And I left him as fast as I could so as to be able to think about it at leisure: the licentiousness was by no means one-sided;

Frederick was proving far more effectual than I had imagined, he did not beat about the bush, he took the bull by the horns and carried out his plans ruthlessly. And, what was more, behind my back, all on his own! Nothing got in his way, not even his pathetic discussion with Albert about Amelia's death—he acted. And the problem was to find out whether he had made much progress since then. And how far could one go? As far as he was concerned the problem of limits was particularly tricky—especially since it involved me too. I was afraid. It was evening again, the barely perceptible disappearance of light, the gradual deepening of the dark shades, the sudden expansion of the holes and corners that fills the thick flux of night. . . The sun had disappeared behind the trees. I remembered having left a book on the terrace so I went to get it. . . and in the book I found an unaddressed envelope enclosing a messily scribbled letter in pencil:

I am writing to establish contact. I do not want to be on my own.

If you are alone you can never be quite sure, for example, whether you have gone mad. For two—it is quite different. For two there is a certitude and an objective guarantee. For two there is no insanity!

It is not that I fear it. I could never go mad. Even if I wanted to. It is absolutely impossible for me because I am anti-madness. I want to insure myself against another risk, possibly even more dangerous, that is to say against a certain anomaly, I might say a certain multiplication of possibilities which threatens us as we stray from the only permissible path. . . Do you understand? I have no time to be more precise. If I were to visit other planets, even if it were only the moon, I would rather be with somebody—as a precaution, so that my humanity should have some mirror to look into.

I will write to you again to keep you informed. Strictly confidential—unofficial—concealed from ourselves; please burn this letter and do not mention it to anyone, not even to me. As though nothing had happened. What is the point in provoking—whom? ourselves? It is better to be discreet.

All in all I think it is for the best that you should have seen the incident on the island. Two pairs of eyes are better than one. To hell with the whole thing! Instead of being aroused and excited by this act they play it coldly, like actors. . . for me, on my orders, and if anyone excites them it is me! What rotten luck! You know how it is, you have seen them. But don't worry. We will manage to excite them.

You have seen it, but now you must bring Albert to the show. HE MUST SEE IT! Tell him that: 1) as you were taking a stroll you happened to surprise their meeting in the garden; 2) you consider it your duty to tell him; 3) they do not know you saw them. You must take him to the show tomorrow, and you must arrange for him to see them and not me. I will work it out to the last detail and write to you. You will receive further instructions. Absolutely. That is very important! Tomorrow! He must know, he must see!

You want to know my plans? I have none. I follow the lines of force, you understand? The lines of desire. I now want him to see them and them to know they have been seen. They must be steeped in guilt. We will see about the rest later.

Please do this. Please do not write back. I shall leave the letters on the wall, near the gate, under a brick. Burn them. And the other one, number 2, Olek, where does he fit

*in, how, in what scheme can he be combined with them,
for it all to run smoothly? He is made to measure for it,
but however much I rack my brains I cannot see how. Little
by little it will take shape and I will succeed in fitting him
in, but for the moment we must just go ahead! Please obey
all my instructions.*

This letter scalded me! I began to pace my room and
finally took it outside. I was greeted by the torpor of the
sleepy earth, the contour of the hills against the fleeting
sky, the tension of everything increased, as it does at night-
fall. A landscape I well knew, that I was certain was going
to be here—but the letter expelled me from every landscape, yes, that's right, it expelled me and I wondered what
to do, what to do? What should I do? Albert, Albert—but
no, that was impossible, I would never be able to do that,
it could never be done. With horror I saw the nebula of a
fantastic desire materialize in a fact, a concrete fact, there
in my pocket, this formal demand. What if Frederick had
gone mad? Was it not to stand security for his madness that
he needed me? It was the ideal moment to desert him—and
I already envisaged a very simple solution which I could
discuss with Albert and Hippo. . . I already saw myself telling them: "Look, a very awkward thing has happened. . .
I'm afraid Frederick. . . is having some psychological
disturbance. . . I've been observing him for some time. . .
you know, after all we've been through it's not surprising. . .
he's not the only one. . . But we ought to look out—I've got
a feeling it's some obsession, some erotic obsession connected with Henia and Karol. . . " That was what I would
tell them. Each word would reject him from the community
of normal men and make him into a lunatic—and all this
would happen behind his back—he would gradually become the object of our discreet care and supervision. He

would not know about it—and, not knowing anything, he would be unable to defend himself—and, from a demon he would slowly turn into a lunatic—that was all. While I returned to stability. It was not too late. I had not yet done anything that could have compromised me, this letter was the first sign of our connivance. . . That was why it scalded me. I had to make a decision. Returning to the house, while the trees above me, their foliage lost in the dark, developed a halo of unreality, I bore my decision to render him inoffensive by casting him into the sphere of pure and simple madness. But a brick by the gate attracted my attention—I glanced at it: another letter awaited me.

The worm! You know about it! You understood it! You must have felt it then as I did.

The worm is Albert! They were united over the worm! They will unite over Albert! They will trample on him.

They do not want to go together? They do not want to? You wait and see, we will soon turn Albert into a soft bed on which they will fornicate.

Albert must be dragged in, he must: 1) see them. To be continued.

I took the letter up to my room and did not read it before I got there. The humiliating part was that it was as familiar to me as if I had written it myself. Yes, Albert had to be that worm, trampled on by them both, he had to provide sin for them, make them guilty, precipitate them into the burning night. But what in fact was the obstacle? Why did they NOT WANT to go together? Ah, I knew—no, I did not know—I could not seize that youthful quality which escapes the adult mind. . . it must have been some sort of continence, a morality, a law, yes, some inner prohibition they were obeying. . . so Frederick was probably right in thinking that it would be enough for them to trample on Albert, to deprave themselves on Albert, for all the brakes to be released! When they became lovers for Albert. . . they would really become lovers. For us, who were too old, it was the only possibility of an erotic contact with them. . . We had to precipitate them into this sin! If they were to dive into it with us we could hope for contact and union! I realized that! And I knew this sin would not tarnish their beauty, on the contrary, their youth, their freshness, would be even more exuberant when they were blackened, dragged by our withered hands into depravity and united with us! Yes! I knew it! Enough of this docile, good-natured youth! We had to create another one, tragically united to us, the adults.

Enthusiasm! Was I not enthusiastic about this prospect? Yes, of course. I, who was already excluded from all beauty, denied entrance to the shimmering net of seduction—unseductive, incapable of charming, indifferent to nature. . . ah, and yet I was still capable of enthusiasm, but I knew that my enthusiasm would never again fill anyone else with enthusiasm. . . and I only took part in life like a whipped and mangy cur. . . But when at that age we are offered the opportunity of touching that flowering season, of entering youth even at the price of depravity, and if it appears that ugliness can still be used and absorbed by beauty, well. . . A temptation sweeping aside all obstacles, insurmountable! Enthusiasm, yes, what am I saying? folly, stifling, but on the other hand. . . No, it was mad! Quite unsuitable! Too personal, too private, and too unusual—and then it was without a precedent! Take this demonic path, this particular path with him, with a being whom I fear and whose extremism I knew would take me too far!

And, like Mephistopheles, ruin Albert's love? No, away, stupid, base fantasy! I do that? For nothing on earth, never!

Then what? Retreat, go to Hippolytus and Albert, make it into a clinical case, turn the devil into a lunatic, hell into an asylum. . . and I was about to proceed and once and for all extirpate this raging iniquity. Raging? Where? What was he doing now? The idea that he should be doing something behind my back pushed me up like a spring and dragged me outside. The dogs bounded up—nobody, nothing but the dark outline of the house came into being before me and stood there like a fact. The lights were on in the kitchen windows. And on the first floor, in the windows of Siemian's room (I had forgotten about him). Myself, before the house, suddenly overwhelmed by the distance of the starry vault, lost among the trees. I hesitated, I trembled. A little further away was the gate, and the loose brick next to it. I went up to it, out of a sense of duty, and when I got there I looked around. . . was he watching me from the bushes? Under the brick, another letter. His inspiration was inexhaustible.

Have you really understood me?
I have already spotted a number of little things.
1) RIDDLE: *Why don't they want to go together?. . .*
Well? Do you know?
I know. Because it would be too FULL *for them. Too* COMPLETE.
FULLNESS *and its antithesis! That which is not achieved, that's the key!*
Great God! Thou art fullness! But this is more wonderful than Thou and I hereby deny Thee.
2) RIDDLE: *Why do they stick to us? Why do they flirt with us?*
Because they want to go through us. Through us. And through Albert. Through us, my dear Witold, my dear

friend, yes. They can only go through us. That is why they are so sweet to us.

Have you ever known anything like it? That they should need us to do it?

3) Do you know what the danger is? That I am at the height of my intellectual and moral powers, and find myself in light, inexpert hands which are still growing. Good God! They are still growing. And they are lightly, lightly, super-ficially introducing me to something which must totally exhaust me intellectually and spiritually. They will hand me this cup lightly, this cup I shall have to drain to the dregs. . .

I have always known something like this was awaiting me. I am Christ crucified on a sixteen-year-old cross. Fare-well! We shall see each other in Golgotha. Farewell!

His inspiration was inexhaustible! I was once again sitting in my room by the lamp. Betray him? Give him up? At the same time I would have had to betray myself and give my-self up!

Myself!

He was not the only one to have thought of all this. I was involved. Appear as a lunatic myself? Betray in myself the only possibility of entering, of entering. . . what? What? What was that? I heard the dinner gong. When I found myself at the table, in the combination we formed every eve-ning, the everyday problems returned, the war and the Ger-mans, the country and the worries, but I felt they were coming from very far away. . . in short, they were no longer my problems.

Frederick was sitting here too, at his place—and dis-cussed, as he ate his ravioli and cheese, the military situa-tion on the various fronts. On several occasions he turned to me and asked my opinion.

10

Albert's initiation went according to plan. Nothing unforeseen happened to complicate it—it ran without a hitch.

I told him "I had something to show him." I led him to the canal, to the appointed place from where the clearing could be seen between the trees. At this point the water in the canal was quite deep—a necessary precaution to prevent him from crossing over to the island and discovering Frederick.

I pointed to the scene.

This was what Frederick had devised in his honor: Karol under the tree, she behind him, both looking up at something in the tree, a bird, perhaps. He raised his hand. And she raised her hand.

Over their heads their hands touched "accidentally." And as they touched they pulled them down abruptly and violently. For some time they both gazed attentively at their joined hands. Then they suddenly fell down—it was impossible to tell who had been pushed by whom—it looked as though their hands had pushed them down.

They fell down, for a moment they lay next to each other and then jumped up. . . and again they stood there as though they did not know what to do next. Slowly she walked away, with him behind her, and they disappeared into the bushes.

A highly refined scene, despite its apparent simplicity. Because the artlessness with which they joined hands experienced an unexpected shock—this sudden fall to the ground—the naturalness of it was convulsed abruptly, departed so violently from normality that for a split second they looked like puppets at the mercy of an elementary force. But that only lasted a second and the way they got up and walked off calmly and deliberately made one suppose they were used to it. That it was not the first time. That they were accustomed to these falls.

The fumes of the canal. The stifling humidity. The motionless frogs. It was five o'clock. The garden was exhausted. The heat.

"Why did you bring me here?"

He asked me the question on our way back to the house. I replied:

"I considered it my duty."

He pondered.

"Thank you."

As we were already within sight of the house, he added: "I don't think it's of much importance. . . But I'm very grateful to you for having drawn my attention to it. . . I'll mention it to Henia."

That was all. He went up to his room. I remained alone, disappointed as one always is when something is realized— because realization is always indistinct, insufficiently precise, with neither the greatness nor the purity of the intention. Having performed my task I suddenly felt useless —what could I do?—literally drained by the event I had just given birth to. The night was falling. Again the night was falling. I went out to get some air and walk along the edge of the fields, my head down; at my feet the earth was simple, submissive, and silent. On my way back I went to have a look under the brick, but nothing awaited me, only the brick, black with humidity, and cool. I followed the path to the house and I stopped, not having the courage to enter the circle of his sinister intrigues. But at the same time the heat of their embrace, of their precocious, excited blood, of their secret contact, enveloped me in such a glow that I burst into the house almost breaking in the door, to continue to live through my dream! I burst in. But here I was to have one of those surprises that spring on you only too frequently. . .

Hippolytus, Frederick, and Albert were in the study—they called to me.

Thinking that this congress was connected with the events on the island I advanced cautiously. . . but at the last moment I had a sort of premonition that it was to do with something else. Hippolytus was seated morosely at his desk and opened his eyes wide when he saw me. Albert was pacing up and down. Frederick was sprawled in an armchair. There was silence. Albert said:

"We must tell Witold."

"They want to liquidate Siemian," said Hippolytus, in a slightly evasive manner.

I still do not understand anything. Explanations followed, which introduced me to the new situation—and again I felt the theatrical quality of patriotic conspiracy—Hippolytus himself must have had this impression too, because his voice became hard and slightly arrogant. And strict. So I discovered that during the night Siemian had had a talk with "some people from Warsaw" in order to establish the details of an action he was supposed to organize in the area. But in the course of the discussion "an odd thing happened, my dear sir," because apparently Siemian said that he was not going to organize this action or any other action, that he had had enough of the whole thing and was withdrawing once and for all from conspiracy, that he was "going home." An odd thing, indeed! There was a row, they started shouting at him and finally, at the end of his tether, he told them he had done what he could and could do no more—"he had lost his nerve"—"his courage had turned to fear" and: "Leave me alone, something's snapped inside me, I'm scared, I don't even know why." He did not feel he could do it any more, it would be the height of irresponsibility to entrust him with anything in these circumstances, he was giving them a loyal warning and asked to be relieved of his duties. That was the last straw! After a violent argument an initially vague suspicion began to take shape: either Siemian had gone mad or he was on the verge of a nervous breakdown. Then they were panic-stricken by the idea that a certain secret they had disclosed to him was no longer in safe hands, that he might well reveal it. . . And, for various reasons, this took on the aspect of a catastrophe, a defeat, a universal disaster, and it was like this, in this tension and excitement, that the terrified and terrifying decision to liquidate him burst into being. Hippo said that they had wanted to follow Siemian into his room at once and "do him in"—but that he had succeeded in extorting a reprieve until the next night, persuading them of the necessity of working out a technical plan so as not to endanger the inhabitants of the home. They agreed on a reprieve, but only for twenty-four hours. They were afraid he might get wind of their plan and escape. Poworna was the best place for them to execute this deed because Siemian had come here in dead secrecy and it would not occur to anybody to look for him here. They finally agreed to return that night to "settle it."

Why did the truth of our struggle against the enemy and the aggressor have to appear in this ridiculous guise—how humiliating and unbearable!—like something out of an old melodrama, but stained with blood and death, a real death!

In order to have a better idea of the new situation and to get used to it I asked: "What's he doing now?" Hippolytus replied:

"He's upstairs. In his room. He's locked himself in. He asked me for horses to go home. But I can't let him have any horses."

And he whispered to himself:

"I can't let him have any horses."

Of course he could not. And yet we could not do something like this—we could not just liquidate somebody, kill a man without leaving any traces, without a verdict, without formalities, without any document! But that was none of our business. We spoke like people stricken by misfortune. But when I asked them what they intended to do the reply lashed out, almost insolently: "What d'you think? The only thing! Obey!"

Hippolytus' tone of voice showed up the sinister change in our relationship. I was no longer his guest, I was on duty, united with them in the severity and cruelty which was aimed at us just as much as at Siemian. What had he done to us? Suddenly, from one day to the other, we had to kill him, risking our own necks!

"Right now there's nothing to be done. They're coming back at half-past twelve at night. I've sent the night watchman to Ostrowiec on a supposedly urgent errand. I'll keep the dogs chained up. All I'm going to do is to show them up and then it's up to them. I've made one condition—no noise, or they'll wake the whole house. As for the body, it'll be removed. . . I've already worked that out. . . in the barn. Tomorrow one of us will pretend to take Siemian to the station, and that'll be that. If they don't make a noise it can all go quite smoothly and not a living soul will suspect a thing. . . "

Frederick asked: "In the old barn, behind the shed?"

He asked the question bluntly, like a conspirator, an agent. And in spite of everything I felt relieved that he should have been mobilized like that, like a conscripted drunkard. But would he have another drink? And suddenly this new adventure struck me as being infinitely more healthy, more decent than what we had been doing until then. But this feeling of relief did not last long.

Immediately after dinner (eaten in the absence of Siemian who had been "indisposed" for a few days and who ate his meals in his room) I went to the gate, just to be sure, and, sure enough, a piece of paper shimmered under the brick.

A complication. What a bore the whole business is! We shall have to wait. Quiet, hush!

We shall have to see how and what. How things are going to turn out. If there's a row and we have to clear off to Warsaw, for instance, and they have to go somewhere else, well, nothing doing. The whole thing will be messed up.

But this may not happen.

You have to know the old whore. You know who I mean? Nature. When she creeps up alongside with something unexpected you must not protest, you must not resist, you must obey, make the best of it, faire bonne mine. . . but in our heart of hearts we must not let go, we must not lose sight of our end, so she can know that we are pursuing our own end. To start with, her attacks are very direct and determined, but afterward it is as though she were to lose interest, she releases her grip and you can return secretly to your own work and even reckon on her being fairly indulgent. . . Look out! Copy my behavior. So there will not be any discrepancies. I shall write to you. This letter must be burned.

This letter! . . . this letter which was even more insane than the ones before it—and yet I understood this insanity so well! It was so legible! These *tactics* he used in his dealings with Nature—they were not unfamiliar to me. And it was obvious that he never let his end out of sight for a minute; this letter showed that he would not give way, that he was faithful to the plan he had conceived and, under the appearance of submission, it concealed an appeal to resistance and obstinacy. And who knows whether it was written for me or for Her—so that she should know that we were not going to give up—and I was only a go-between? I suddenly thought about it: how strange that every word, every movement of Frederick's only seemed to refer to whomever they were addressed, while he continued his inexhaustible dialogue with the Power. . . a cunning dialogue where the truth seemed the lie, and the lie the truth. Oh, how hard he pretended in this letter to act behind Nature's back, while in fact he was writing it to keep her informed! He obviously thought this strategy would disarm her, amuse her perhaps. . . We spent the rest of the evening waiting. From time to time somebody surreptitiously glanced at the clock. The lamp hardly lit the room. Henia, as usual, was huddled next to Albert; he, as he did every evening, had put his arm around her shoulders and I discovered that the "island" had in no way changed his behavior toward her. He was impenetrable and I wondered how much he was worrying about Siemian and if he noticed the noise Karol was making as he shifted and arranged some large crates. Maria was sewing (like the "children," she had not been let into the secret). Frederick, his legs outstretched, his arms resting on the arms of the chair. Hippolytus sitting gazing into space. Our tension began to be enveloped by exhaustion.

United by Siemian, by this secret mission which had

been assigned to us, we, the men, formed a group apart. Henia asked: "What are you doing with those crates, Karol?" "Don't you get in my way!" he replied. Their voices rang out in the silence and we could not understand what they meant, what they were trying to do—we did not say a word.

At eleven they went to bed, as did Maria, and we, the men, began to make the necessary preparations. Hippolytus brought out some shovels, a large sack, and a coil of rope. Frederick cleaned the gun as a precaution, Albert and I made a tour of inspection around the house. All the lights were out except in one window on the first floor—Siemian's —where it shone through a thin curtain in a pale halo of light and fear, fear and light. What could have happened to make his courage turn to fear so suddenly? What could have happened to make him lose his nerve overnight? A Resistance leader turn into a coward! What an odd thing! Suddenly the house seemed to me to contain two forms of insanity, with Siemian on the first floor and Frederick on the ground floor (playing his game with Nature). . . they were both cornered, driven to their limit. On my way back to the house I almost burst out laughing at the sight of Hippo examining two kitchen knives and testing their blades. Good God! This poor old fat man, transformed into a murderer preparing for the slaughter, was a buffoonery. And suddenly the absurdity of our situation, so clumsily immersed in this murder, made these preparations look like a play acted by a group of amateurs, far more comic than dangerous. Anyhow, all this was only being done *as a precaution*, there was nothing decisive about it. But at the same time the glint of the knife seemed to have something irrevocable: the die was cast, the knife had already appeared!

Olek. . . Frederick's eyes, staring at the knife, showed

that he was thinking about it too, there could be no doubt. Olek. . . A knife. . . . Identical to the other, the one which stabbed Amelia, almost the same, here, among us—ah, this knife connected us to the other crime, it evoked it inexorably, it marked its beginning in some way—hanging here, now, over our heads. A strange analogy, a curious repetition! The knife. Albert was also staring at it attentively—and so both of them, Frederick and Albert, had taken a mental grip on this knife, each one in view of his own ends. But since they were on duty, in action, they withdrew into themselves—and we continued our preparations and waited.

We had to perform this task fully—but we were so exhausted, so fed up with this melodrama of history, we thirsted for fresh air! After midnight Hippo left the house on tiptoe to meet the fellows from the A.K. Albert went up to the first floor to guard Siemian's door—I remained downstairs with Frederick and never have I found a tête-à-tête so oppressive. I knew he had something to say to me, but we were not allowed to speak—so he remained silent—and although nobody was there to overhear us we behaved like strangers; it was these precautions that evoked out of thin air a third mysterious presence, inexplicable and obstinate. And opposite me his face—so familiar, that of an accomplice—walled in and inaccessible. . . Next to one another we existed, that was all, we just existed and nothing else, but we soon heard the heavy steps and hard breathing of Hippo on his way back to the house. He was alone. What had happened? More complications! Something had gone wrong. Panic. The people he had arranged to meet had not come to the appointment. Somebody else had turned up instead of them and left almost immediately. As for Siemian, Hippo said:

"It's up to us. They can't do it, they've had to clear off in a hurry. That's the order."

In Hippo's voice was complete determination; it was an order not to let him escape on any account, the lives of several people depended on it and we had no right to take any risks; it was an order, no, not a written one, there was no time for that, there was no time anyhow, that was all, he just had to be liquidated! We had been assigned that task. Such was the order, brutal, panic-stricken, the product of a tense situation we could not know about. Doubt it? That would have been to assume the responsibility for all consequences, and that could be catastrophic. After all, we would not have resorted to such drastic expedients without good reason. And any resistance on our side would have looked like flight—at a moment when we wanted to be ready for action. In these circumstances we could not allow ourselves to be in any way weak, and, if Hippo had led us straight to Siemian's room we would very probably have settled it in one go. But these unexpected complications gave us the excuse for putting off the operation until the next night. Because the parts had to be distributed, because we had to get ready and take the necessary precautions. . . and it turned out to be preferable if we could do it the next night. . . I was told to guard Siemian's door until dawn, when I was to be relieved by Albert, and we wished one another good night, because, in spite of everything, we retained our good manners. Hippolytus went off to his bedroom carrying the lamp and we were still on the staircase when a figure moved in the dark suite of rooms. Albert had a torch and flashed a ray of white light. Karol. In his shirt.

"Where have you been? What are you doing at this time of night?" shouted Albert, unable to control his nervous agitation.

"I was in the bathroom."

That could have been true. And Albert would certainly
not have let out such a groan of anguish if he himself had
not shown up the boy with the ray of his own torch. But as
he showed him up he groaned aloud. This groan astounded
us. And we were no less astonished by the almost vulgar
and provocative tone of Karol's:

"What d'you want?"

He was prepared to hit him. Henia's fiancé switched off
his torch at once. "I'm sorry," we heard in the dark, "I
just wondered."

And he walked away rapidly, in the dark.

I did not have to leave my room to guard Siemian's door—
our rooms were adjoining. He made no noise, but he had
left the light on. I did not lie down for fear of falling asleep.
I sat at my table and in my head I could still feel the
frantic rush of the recent events which I could neither control nor understand because, over the material course of
things, spread a mystical sphere of accents and meanings,
like the gleam of the sun on troubled waters. I sat for over
an hour, lost in the contemplation of this glittering flow,
before I noticed a piece of paper that had been slipped
under my door.

*Apropos of the last short circuit A.—K. Did you see how
his fury exploded? K. wanted to hit him.*

They already know he has seen them. That is why.

*They already know because I told them. I told them you
told me Albert told you—that he had surprised them on
the island. That he had seen them (but not me) quite by
chance as he was going for a walk in the garden.*

*As you can well believe they laughed, that is they
laughed* together *because I told them both and, being together, they could do nothing but laugh. . . because they
were* together *and, what is more, in front of me! Now they*

are already ESTABLISHED *as* A.'s laughing executioners. *Only as long as they are together, of course, as long as they form a couple, as long as they are a couple—because, you saw what happened at dinner, she, as far as she is she, that is, on her own, is faithful to her fiancé. But together they laugh at him.*

And now the KNIFE.

The knife creates a new formula, s. (Siemian)—s¹ (Skuziak).

*Which makes: (ss¹)—*A., *through* A., *through Amelia's murder.*

But at the same time there is A.—KH. *Or* (KH.)—(ss¹).

What chemistry! It is all connected. As yet the connections are obscure, but you can already spot a TENDENCY *in this direction. . . And to think that I did not know how to fit Skuziak into the game—and he enters it on his own via the* KNIFE. *But be careful! Do not upset anything. We must not force. . . we must not impose ourselves. . . let us drift with the tide as though nothing had happened and just take every chance to get nearer to our end.*

We must collaborate in Hippo's underground action. Without revealing that our underground action has another aim. Pretend to be up to your neck in the national struggle, in the A.K., in the Poland-Germany dilemma, as though that were what it was about. . . while in fact it is only about making:

HENIA WITH KAROL.

But we cannot let that be seen. We cannot let that be seen by anyone. We must not give ourselves away. Not a word to anyone. Not even between ourselves, we are not allowed to mention it. Above all no alarm. Quiet. It must work itself out. . .

We need courage and determination to proceed with our venture even if it should look like a licentious obscenity.

Obscenity ceases being obscene if we persevere! We must push on because if we give way the obscenity will crush us. Do not be discouraged, do not betray! There is no return. Best wishes. Your obedient servant. Burn this letter, huh!

"Burn this letter, huh!" he ordered. But he had already said: "IT IS ONLY ABOUT MAKING: HENIA WITH KAROL." Who was this letter written to? To me? Or to Her, to Nature?

There was a knock at my door.

"Come in."

It was Albert.

"May I speak to you?"

I offered him my chair, and he sat down. I sat on the bed.

"I do apologize and I know you're tired. But I've just realized that I won't be able to sleep a wink tonight before I've had a talk with you. Different from the other ones. More frank. I hope you won't be annoyed. You can imagine why I'm here. It's about. . . the business on the island."

"I don't think I can be of much use to you. . . "

"I know. I know. Forgive me for interrupting you. I know you don't know anything. But I'd like to know what you think. I can't put my ideas straight. What do you think about it? What do you think about it?"

"Me? What can I think about it? I pointed it out to you because I considered it my du. . . "

"Of course. And I'm most grateful to you. I really don't know how to thank you. But I'd like to know your point of view. In my opinion it's of no importance, because they've known each other since they were children. . . It's more childish than anything else. . . And at that age! There was probably something between them some time ago. . . most likely. . . you know, those infantile jokes and caresses— strange, isn't it? And now they occasionally do it again. A sort of sprouting, budding sensuality. And then it could also have been an optical illusion, since we were quite far away, behind the bushes. I can't doubt Henia's feelings for me. I have no right, no reason to do so. I know she loves me. Anyhow, how could I compare our love to these—childish pranks? Ridiculous!"

His body! He was sitting opposite me. His body! He was in a dressing gown—with his corpulent, pampered, chubby, pale, clean, and dressing-gowned body! He was sitting with this body as if with a bag or a travel kit. His body! Infuriated by this body and become carnal in my turn, I looked at him mockingly, I mocked him outright, almost with a whistle. Not an atom of pity. His body!

"Believe me if you can, but I assure you I would never have thought twice about it. . . But one thing worries me. I don't know, I may have been deceived. . . That's why I wanted to ask you. I apologize at the start if this were to seem. . . at all fanciful. I admit I don't even know how to put it. What they were doing. . . you know, when they suddenly fell down and then got up. . . you'll agree it was rather. . . peculiar. One doesn't do it *like that!*"

He stopped, swallowed and seemed ashamed of having swallowed.

"Is that the impression you had?"

"No, it didn't seem normal. You see, they could have kissed, but normally. . . If, for instance, he had pushed her over—normally. Even if he had had her in front of me. . . it wouldn't have upset me. . . so much. . . as those odd movements. . ."

He took my hand. He looked me in the eyes. I felt sick. I started to hate him.

"Please tell me frankly, am I right? Maybe I didn't see it as I should have seen it? Maybe this strangeness is something in myself? I don't know any more. Tell me, please!"

His body!

Skillfully concealing my quivering but pitiless malice I said—hardly anything—but hardly anything was enough to add fuel to the fire: "How should I know?. . . But I suppose. . . Maybe, up to a point. . . "

"But I don't know how much importance I should attribute to it! Is it serious? And how far? First of all, tell me: do you think that he and she. . . "

"What?"

"Forgive me. I was thinking of sex appeal. What we call sex appeal. When I saw them together for the first time I noticed it at once. Sex appeal. Attraction. Sexual attraction. Him and her. But then, when I started feeling something for her, it faded into the background, compared with what I felt it was meaningless. I stopped thinking about it. It was so childish! It's only now. . . "

He sighed.

"Now I'm afraid it might be—still worse than I could ever have imagined."

He got up.

"They fell onto the ground. . . but not as they should have fallen. They got up almost immediately—not as they should have got up, either. And then they walked away, and that wasn't as they should have walked away! What is it? What is it hiding? One doesn't do it *like that!*"

He sat down again.

"Well? Well? What can that mean?"

He looked at me.

"You have no idea how this is torturing me! Say something! Say something, for heaven's sake! Don't leave me all alone—with that!" He gave me a pale smile. "Please forgive me."

So he too was after my company and preferred not to "be alone with it"—I was decidedly in fashion! But unlike Frederick he implored me not to confirm his folly and waited with his heart in his mouth for my denial which would reduce everything to a chimera. He depended on me to calm him. . . His body! And my prodigious lightness! To sentence him to hell I hardly had to make any effort, all I had to do, as I had just done, was to mumble a few vague phrases: "To tell the truth. . . It could be. . . I must admit. . . Perhaps. . . " I said them. He replied:

"She loves me, I know she loves me, I'm certain she loves me!"

He was defending himself in spite of everything.

"She loves you? No doubt. But don't you think that between them love is superfluous? Love is necessary with you, not with him."

His body!

For a long time he said nothing. He sat in silence. I too sat in silence. Silence enveloped us. Frederick? Was he asleep? And Siemian? And Olek in the lumber room? What was he doing? Was he asleep? The house seemed harnessed to masses of horses, each one charging in a different direction.

He smiled awkwardly:

"It really is distressing," he said. "I've just lost my mother. And now. . . "

He mused.

"I really don't know how to apologize for this nocturnal visit. Alone, it was unbearable. I'd like to say something else to you, if you don't mind. Look. Sometimes I myself am amazed. . . that she should feel something for me. What I feel for her is another matter. I feel what I feel for her because she's made for love, to be loved. But what can she love in me? My feeling, my love for her? No, not only that, she loves *me too*—but why? What does she love in me? You see what I'm like. I'm under no illusions. I don't particularly like myself, and I really can't conceive, can't begin to understand what she can see in me, and I must admit I'm rather shocked by it. If I had to reproach her for something it would be precisely. . . for accepting me so eagerly. Will you believe me if I tell you that in the moment of most violent ecstasy I resent her for this ecstasy, for giving in to it with me? And I've never felt at ease with her, I always had the impression of a favor, of a concession granted to me, I even had to resort to cynicism to benefit from these "facilities," this astonishing favor of nature. Very well. But apart from this—she loves me. It's a fact. Deserved or undeserved, favor or not, she loves me."

"She loves you. No doubt about it."

"Wait! I know what you're going to say: that the other business is beyond love, in another sphere. Quite right! And this is why my position is so. . . barbarous and immoral, so refined in its cruelty—One wonders how it could have gone so far. If she were to be unfaithful to me. . .

"My bride is doing it with. . . with. . . someone like that," he suddenly said in another tone, and looked at me. "What does that mean? And how can I defend myself? What can I do?

"She's doing it with. . . " he went on, "and in a strange. . . exclusive. . . unknown way, which hurts me, which stabs me to the bone, because you know, I can feel this taste, I'm catching it. . . Will you believe it, but on the basis of the sample we saw I've reconstructed *every* possibility between them, the totality of their mutual behavior. And it is so. . . ingeniously erotic that I can't imagine who can have thought it up! It's like a dream! Who invented it? He or she? If she did—she's an artist!"

After a moment:

"And do you know what I think? That he's never had her. And that that's far more terrible than if they were sleeping together. An idea like that is sheer lunacy, isn't it? And yet! Because if he'd had her I would at least have been able to defend myself, while there. . . I can't. . . and I don't know if she belongs more to him simply because he never had her. Because everything happens differently in them! It's different! It's different!"

Ha! He did not know the most important part. That what he had seen on the island existed *for* Frederick and *through* Frederick—it was a sort of bastard born from them and Frederick. And how satisfying to be able to keep him in ignorance, that he should never for a moment suspect that I, his confidant, was on the side of his persecutors, of the element that was destroying him! Although it was not my element (they were too young). Although I was his comrade and not theirs—and as I destroyed him I destroyed myself. But. . . this extraordinary lightness.

"It's the war that does that," he said. "It's the war. But why must I be at war with brats! One of them murdered my mother and the other. . . It's too much, this time it's too much. It's really gone too far. Do you want to know what I'm going to do?"

Since I did not reply, he repeated emphatically:

"Do you know what I intend to do?"

"I'm listening. Tell me."

"I won't surrender an inch of ground."

"Really?"

"I won't allow her to be seduced—and I won't allow myself to be seduced."

"What do you mean by that?"

"I'll be able to defend and look after my own interests. I love her. She loves me. That's all that matters. The rest must yield, the rest must be meaningless, because that's how I want it. Because I'll be able to want it. You know, I don't actually believe in God. My mother did, but not I. But I want God to exist. In this case too I'll be able to want, and will impose my rights and my morals. . . I shall call Henia to order. I haven't spoken to her yet, but I'll do so tomorrow and I'll bring her to her senses."

"What will you say to her?"

"I shall behave decently and force her to behave decently. I shall behave respectfully—I'll respect her and make her respect me. I shall treat her in such a way that she won't be able to deny me her love or her fidelity. I firmly believe, you know, that respect and consideration create reciprocal obligations. And I shall behave correctly toward this brat, too. Just now he almost made me fly off the handle—but this won't happen again."

"You want to behave. . . responsibly?"

"That's just what I meant! Responsibly! I'll make them behave responsibly!"

"Yes, but 'responsibly' implies seriousness, 'importance.' Someone who's responsible only thinks about what's important. And what is the most important thing? It might be one thing for you and another for them. Everyone chooses in accordance with his taste and opinion."

"How do you mean? I'm responsible, not they. How could they be responsible? If it's all a lot of childish nonsense. Nonsense!"

"And what if—for them—childishness were to be more important?"

"What? What's important for me must be important for them. What do they know? I know more. I'll force them! I'm more important than they, you can't deny that; my common sense must prevail!"

"Just a minute. I thought you considered yourself more important because of your principles. . . but it now seems that your principles are more important because you yourself are more important. Personally. As a man. As an adult."

"Whichever way you look at it!" he shouted. "It's six of one and half a dozen of the other! Please excuse me again.

These confidences so late at night. . . Thank you so much."

He went out. I wanted to roar with laughter. Well! He had swallowed the bait—and was now writhing like a fish out of water!

That was a fine trick our little couple had played!

He was suffering. Was he suffering? Of course he was suffering, but a chubby—tired—bald suffering. . .

Charm was on the other bank. So I too was on the other bank. Everything that came from over there had something seductive, enchanting, voluptuous. . . His body!

This lout who pretended to defend morals and was in fact crushing them with his own weight! He wanted to crush them. He forced his morals on them for the sole reason that they were "his"—that they were heavier, older, and more developed. . . the morals of an adult. He forced them on them.

A real lout! I hated him. Only. . . was I not a little like him? I, an adult. . . That was what I was thinking about when there was another knock on the door. I was sure it was Albert who had forgotten to say something—but it was Siemian! I almost choked in his face with surprise—he was the last person I expected!

"I'm sorry to disturb you, but I heard voices and knew you weren't asleep. May I have a glass of water?"

He drank it slowly, in little sips, without looking at me. He had no tie, his shirt was open and creased, he had put on some brilliantine but his hair was on end and he kept on passing his fingers through it. He drank the water but did not leave. He stood in the middle of the room passing his hand through his hair.

"What an arabesque!" he muttered. "Unbelievable. . . "

He stood there, as though he were alone. Intentionally I said nothing. He murmured, not to me:

"I need help."

"What can I do for you?"

"You realize I'm at the end of my tether, don't you?" he asked me indifferently, as though he were talking about somebody else.

"I must admit. . . I don't quite understand. . . "

"You must be *au courant!*" he laughed. "You know who I am. And that I've lost my nerve."

He ruffled his hair, waiting for an answer. He was in no hurry because he looked thoughtful, or rather as though he were concentrating on some thought without really thinking about it. I decided to discover what he wanted— I told him I was *au courant*. . .

"You're a nice man. . . I couldn't stay in my room next door. . . shut in. . . " He pointed to the room next door. "How can I put it? I decided to appeal to someone. I decided to appeal to you. Maybe because I like you, maybe because our rooms are adjoining. . . I can't be alone any more. I can't stand it. May I sit down?"

He sat down gingerly as though he had just recovered from a long illness, had difficulty in controlling his limbs, and had to work out every movement in advance. "I would like you to tell me something," he said, "is there some sort of plot against me?"

"Why?" I asked.

He decided to laugh, and went on: "I'm sorry, I wanted to talk openly and frankly. . . but first I must tell you in what state of mind I've come to you. I must tell you a few things about my life. Please listen to me as benevolently as you can. Anyhow, you must have heard about me. You heard of me as a brave man, as a dangerous man, I dare say. . . Yes. . . But a short time ago something went wrong. . . I'm in a funk, you see. A little weakness in the pit of my stomach. It's been like that for about a week. I was sitting by the lamp when I suddenly thought: so far you've been lucky. What would happen if something were to go wrong tomorrow and they caught you?"

"You must have thought that before?"

"Of course! Frequently! But this time it was worse—because I suddenly thought of something else—that I shouldn't be thinking this because it could weaken me, make me pervious, or what do you call it?—and attract danger. I told myself it was better not to think about it. And no sooner had I said that than it was too late, I couldn't put the idea out of my head, it took a hold of me, and now I can't think about anything else—something's going to go wrong and I mustn't think about it because then something really will go wrong, and so on, in a vicious circle. What do you think? I'm trapped!"

"Nerves."

"It isn't nerves. Do you know what it is? It's courage turning to fear. There's nothing one can do about it."

He lit a cigarette. He inhaled deeply and blew the smoke out. "Look. Three weeks ago I still had an aim in life, an assignment, a struggle, such and such an objective. . . Now I have nothing. Everything has suddenly slipped down, like my trousers, if you don't mind my saying so. Now I only think of one thing: keeping out of harm's way. And I'm right. Whoever fears for himself is always right! The worst of it is that I am right, for the first time in my life! But what do you want to do to me? I've been here for five days. I ask for horses and they won't let me have any. It's as though you were keeping me in prison. What do you want to do to me? I'm going crazy in my room. Is that what you want?"

"Calm yourself. It's nerves."

"Do you want to finish me off?"

"You're overdoing it."

"I'm not that stupid. I lost my nerve. The trouble is I

was in such a funk I gave myself away. Now they know. As long as I wasn't afraid they weren't afraid of me. Now I'm afraid, I'm dangerous. I understand that. I can't be trusted any more. But I'm appealing to you as a man. I took this decision: to get up and talk to you, man to man. It's my last chance. I've come straight to you because a man in my position has no choice. Listen to me. It's a vicious circle. You're afraid of me because I'm afraid of you, I'm afraid of you because you're afraid of me. I can only get out by taking a leap and that's why I've come to you in the middle of the night, although we don't know each other. . . You're an intelligent man, a writer, try to understand, give me a hand, help me out."

"What can I do?"

"They must let me leave. Get away. That's my only dream. To get away. To withdraw. I could go on foot—but you could catch me in a field, and there. . . Persuade them to let me live, tell them I won't hurt anyone, I've had enough of it, I can't go on. I want to be left in peace. In peace. Once I've got away—it'll be all right. Please, I beg of you, tell them, I can't stand it any more. . . Or help me to escape. I appeal to you because I can't be alone against you all, like an outcast, give me a hand, don't leave me like that. We don't know each other, but I chose you. I came to you. Why do you want to go on persecuting me since I'm already harmless—for good. It's all over!"

I struck the most unexpected rock in the person of this man who had started to tremble. What could I say to him? I was still full of Albert—and I was confronted by this vomiting man—enough, enough, enough!—who begged for pity. In a flash I saw the whole problem that faced me. I could not reject him because his death took shape from his quivering life before me. He had come to me, confided in me, had become, from that alone, close and therefore immense, his life and his death towered high above me. At the same time his appearance—wrenching me from Albert —led me back to duty, to our cause, to our common action under Hippolytus' command and he, Siemian, was nothing but the objective of our action. . . and, as an objective, he was rejected from the sphere of the living. I could neither recognize him nor agree with him, nor speak to him frankly, I had to keep my distance, not let him come too near, maneuver him politically. . . and for a moment my spirit rebelled, like a horse before an insurmountable obstacle. . . because he was appealing to the man in me, wanted to approach me as a man, and I had no right to see a man in him. What could I say to him? The most important thing was not to let him get any closer—not to let him guess what was going on inside me.

"Look," I said, "there is a war on. The country is under occupation. In these circumstances desertion is a luxury we cannot indulge in. Each of us has to watch the other. You know that."

"That means you don't. . . really want to talk to me."

He paused, as though he were savoring the silence that separated us more and more.

"Tell me," he said, "have you ever lost your trousers?"

Once again I did not reply, increasing the distance. "You know," he said patiently, "I've lost everything. . . I've lost my pants. . . I'm stark naked. Let's speak to the point. I've come to see you in the middle of the night like one stranger to another, can't we talk more openly? You don't want to?"

He stopped and waited for me to answer. I said nothing.

"I couldn't care less what you think of me," he added apathetically. "But I've chosen you—as my savior or my murderer. Which do you prefer?"

I then resorted to a blatant lie—as blatant to me as it

was to him—and so I finally rejected him from the sphere
of men: "I'm not aware of your being in any danger. You're
exaggerating. It's your nerves."

This cut the ground from under his feet. He did not say
anything—but he made no attempt to leave, did not move,
stood there—passively. As though I had destroyed all means
of retreat. And I thought this could last forever, he would
not budge, why should he budge? He would stay there. . .
crushing me. I did not know what to do with him and he
could not help me because I had rejected him, cast him out,
and I was without him, facing him—alone. . . He was at my
mercy. But between us there was nothing but indifference,
a cold hostility. He was alien to me, he disgusted me! A
dog, a horse, a chicken, even a maggot would have appealed
to me more than this adult, worn man, with his life history
written on his face—an adult hates adults! Nothing more
disgusting for a man than another man—I mean, of course,
elderly men with their life history written on their faces.
He did not attract me, no! He could not seduce me. He
could not please me! He repelled me like Albert, and even
more—he repelled me as I repelled him and we almost
clashed antlers like two stags—and that I should repel him
in my deterioration simply increased my animosity. First
Albert, now him—both of them horrible! And myself with
them! An adult can only be bearable for another adult as a
renunciation, when he renounces himself to incarnate something else—horror, virtue, the people, the fight. . . But a
man who is nothing but a man—how ghastly!

But he had chosen me. He had chosen me and now
would not leave. He stood motionless before me. I coughed
and this little cough informed me that the situation was
getting worse. His death—however revolting—loomed up
like an inevitable reef.

I had one desire—that he should leave. I would have

plenty of time to think about it afterward, but first he had to leave. Why not tell him I was prepared to help him? I would not be committing myself, I could always turn this promise into a ruse, into a maneuver—if I were to decide to kill him and disclose everything to Hippolytus—; it was in the interest of our own action, of our group, that I should gain his confidence and be able to do what I liked with him. If I were to decide to kill him. . . What harm was there in lying to a man you were going to kill?

"Listen to me. The first thing to do is to control your nerves. That's vital. Come down to lunch tomorrow. Say you've had a nervous breakdown and that it's over. That you'll gradually return to normal. Pretend. As for me I'll talk to Hippolytus and try to arrange for you to leave. Now go back to your room, somebody might come in and find you here. . . "

As I spoke I had no idea what I was saying. Truth or lies? Help or betrayal? We would soon see—in the meantime he had to go! He got to his feet and drew himself up, I did not see a glimmer of hope in his face, nothing flickered, he made no attempt to thank me, even with a glance— knowing there was nothing he could do, that he could only be, be what he was, be this ungrateful, unpleasant existence —whose suppression would be even more revolting. He was blackmailing me with his existence. . . ah, how different it all was from Karol!

Karol!

When he had gone out I started to write to Frederick. It was a report. I told him about my two visits. And it was also a document which confirmed my clear acceptance of our common action. Confirmed it in writing. I established a dialogue.

11

The next day Siemian appeared for lunch.

I had got up late and when I came downstairs they were just about to go in to lunch and that was when Siemian appeared, freshly shaved, his hair oiled and scented, a handkerchief peeping out of his breast pocket. It was the appearance of a corpse—had we not been killing him uninterruptedly for two days? And yet the corpse kissed his hostess' hand with the grace and manners of a cavalry officer and, after having greeted everybody, started to explain that "the indisposition which had kept him in his room was almost over," that he was feeling better and that he was sick of rotting away upstairs in his room "while the entire family was reunited down here." Hippolytus himself drew up a chair for him, another place was laid, our respect for him returned unaltered and he sat down at the table—as superior and oppressive as on the evening he arrived. The soup was brought in. He asked for a glass of vodka. He must have been making a considerable effort: he spoke like a corpse, ate like a corpse, and drank like a corpse—and these activities must have been extorted by fear from the power of his apathy. "I haven't quite recovered my appetite but. . . maybe a little soup. I'd like another vodka too, if I may."

This meal. . . confused, based on a latent force full of uncontrollable crescendos and contradictory meanings, as

157

blurred as one text typed over another. . . ! Albert sitting at
his place next to Henia—and he must have spoken to her
and "conquered her with respect" because they both treated
each other with special consideration and politeness, she
was ennobled, he was ennobled—they were both noble. As
for Frederick, he was as voluble and sociable as ever, but
he was clearly pushed into the background by Siemian, who
had imperceptibly seized control. . . Yes, far more than at
his first appearance we felt obliged to obey and accept with
a sort of inner tension the smallest desire which rose in him
like a plea but struck us like an order. For me, who knew
that it was his misery disguised, out of fear, in his former
superiority which was now dead and buried, the whole thing
seemed a good farce! To start with he concealed his state
of mind under the affability of an officer, a braggart Cos-
sack, but his bitterness soon began to ooze from every pore
together with the cold indifference composed of apathy
which I had noticed the day before. He became visibly more
morose and ugly. He felt confronted by an unbearable
contradiction when, out of fear, he tried to embody for us
the former Siemian, the Siemian he was no more, whom he
feared more than we did, whom he no longer had a right
to be—the former Siemian, the dangerous Siemian, accustomed to giving orders, to using men, to making them kill
each other. "I'd like a little salt. . . oh, thank you!" That
sounded familiar and good-natured, but it was aggressive
and somewhere, in its essence, it was filled with scorn for
other people's existence, and Siemian felt his fear turn into
something terrifying. Frederick, I knew, must have been
particularly receptive to this increase of horror and terror.
But Siemian's game would never have become so impetuous
if Karol had not joined him from the other end of the
table, and had not supported his power with his whole
person.

Karol ate his soup, buttered his bread—but Siemian had instantly assumed control over him as he had on the first evening. The boy had a leader once again. His hands became military and efficient. His whole incomplete being was surrendered to the leader, surrendered and offered up— and if he ate it was to serve him, if he buttered his bread it was with his consent and his head was suddenly submitted to Siemian with his close-cropped hair which curled slightly over his brow. He had no need for words—he had just become like that—as one changes in different lighting. Maybe Siemian had not realized it at once but a special relationship developed between him and the boy and this dark cloud of aggression filled with sovereignty (which was only simulated) began to search for Karol and to concentrate its force on him. Albert looked on, sitting next to Henia, as noble as one could wish. . . Albert imbued with justice, demanding love and virtue. . . watched the leader clouded by the boy, the boy by the leader.

He must have felt this—Albert—that this alliance full of animosity was directed chiefly against the respect which he defended and which defended him because what was being formed between the boy and the leader was nothing but disdain and, above all, disdain for death. If the boy was offering his body and soul to his leader, his life and death, was it not because the leader was not afraid either to die or to kill and could therefore dominate others? This disdain for life and death entailed all the other possibilities of devaluation, whole oceans of devaluation. And the adolescent's capacity for disdain joined the superior nonchalance of the leader—they affirmed each other, fearing neither pain nor death, one because he was a boy, the other because he was the leader. The situation became more tense and vast because it rested on artificial assumptions which are always hard to control—it was only from fear and desire to survive that Siemian was playing the part of a leader. And this part, confirmed by the adolescent, suffocated him, terrified him. Frederick must (I was sure) have been aware of the violent increase of tension among these three people, Siemian, Karol and Albert—an increase which heralded an explosion. . . while Henia was bending calmly over her plate.

Siemian ate. . . to prove he was capable of eating like everyone else. . . and tried to exert his Slavonic charm which was poisoned by his cadaverous coldness, and which, in contact with Karol, was instantly turned to violence and blood. Frederick was all eyes and ears. But it then happened that Karol asked for a glass and Henia handed it to him— and it was just possible that the moment when the glass passed from one hand to the other lasted slightly, very slightly, too long, that Henia had hesitated for a split second before withdrawing her hand. It was possible. But was it true? This insignificant suspicion struck Albert like a mallet —he turned ashen—and Frederick cast a glance at them— an indifferent glance.

The fruit was served. Siemian fell silent. He sat there, becoming more and more disagreeable, as though his store of politeness were exhausted, as though he were from now on determined not to please, as though the doors of horror were now wide open before him. He was cold. Henia started toying with her fork and it happened that Karol touched her fork with his—it was impossible to tell for sure whether he was playing with it or had touched it by chance, and it could have been quite accidental, because the fork was by his hand—but Albert turned ashen again: was it possible that it was by chance? Of course it was possible, and anyhow the matter was so insignificant that it was not worth thinking twice about. But on the other hand it was not impossible. . . yes, maybe this very insignificance allowed them to play this game which was oh! so innocent, so light, so microscopic that (the girl) could play it with (the boy) under the eyes of her fiancé without compromising her virtue—such an inoffensive game. . . And was it not this lightness that tempted them—the fact that the faintest movement of their hands struck Albert a violent blow— maybe they had not been able to resist the temptation of this game, so harmless in itself but so disastrous for Albert. Siemian finished eating his fruit. Even if Karol liked, unconsciously, to torment Albert, the game did not in any way affect his fidelity to Siemian: he played it like a soldier ready to die lightheartedly and blindly. But that too seemed to me curiously uncontrolled, artificial: the game with the forks was an obvious continuation of the fictitious game on the island and this flirtation of theirs was "theatrical." So I found myself at this table between two mystifications, but far more tense than any real situation could have been. An artificial leader and an artificial love.

We got up. Lunch was over.

Siemian went over to Karol.

"Hey there, you little rascal. . . " he said.

"Well?" asked Karol, thrilled.

The officer turned his pale eyes to Hippolytus, cold and disagreeable: "What about having a word together?" he proposed between his teeth.

I wanted to listen to their conversation, but he stopped me with a short: "Not you." What was that? An order? Had he forgotten our talk last night? But I complied with his wish and stayed on the veranda while he went off with Hippolytus into the garden. Henia stood next to Albert and had even taken his arm, as though nothing had happened between them, once again faithful and pure; but Karol who was standing by the open door had also put his hand on it (his hand on the door—Henia's hand on Albert's arm). And the fiancé said to the young lady: "Let us go for a walk." To which she replied, like an echo: "Let us go for a walk." They went down a path and Karol stayed with us, like a bawdy and incomprehensible joke. . . Frederick, looking at the couple and then at Karol, could not help murmuring: "You don't say!" I replied with a furtive smile, addressed to him alone.

Hippolytus came back after a quarter of an hour and called us into the study.

"We must finish him off," he said. "We must do it tonight. He's insisting!"

And sinking into the sofa, he repeated to himself, closing his eyes voluptuously: "He's insisting!"

It transpired that Siemian had again asked for horses— not as a plea but in such terms that Hippolytus could not get over it. "Gentlemen, he's a gangster! He's a murderer! He wanted horses, I told him today was impossible but maybe tomorrow. . . Then he gripped my hand and squeezed it, I tell you, like a real murderer. . . and he said that if the horses weren't ready tomorrow morning at ten o'clock he would. . . He's insisting, I tell you!" he concluded excitedly. "We must get rid of him tonight because tomorrow I'll be *forced* to give him the horses."

And he added softly:

"I'll be forced to. . . "

That was a surprise for me. Obviously Siemian had not been able to sustain the role we had agreed on the night before; instead of talking calmly, conciliatingly, he had threatened. . . he must have been possessed, terrorized by the dangerous ex-Siemian whom he had resuscitated during the meal, hence the threats, the order, the insistence, the cruelty (he could not control this ex-Siemian since he feared him more than anyone else). In short, he had become dangerous again. But at least I no longer felt exclusively responsible for him at present as I had the night before in my room—because I had shifted the matter onto Frederick.

Hippolytus got up: "Well, gentlemen, how are we going to do it? Who?" He produced four matches and broke one of them. I watched Frederick—I expected him to give some sign, should I reveal last night's conversation with Siemian? But he was terribly pale. He swallowed.

"I'm sorry," he said. "I don't know if. . . "

"What?" asked Hippolytus.

"Death," said Frederick briefly. He avoided his eyes. "Mur-der him?"

"What do you mean? It's an order."

"Mur-der him?" he repeated. He did not look at anyone. He was alone with this word. Nobody but him and murder. His chalky pallor betrayed him, because he *knew what it was to murder*. At that moment, he knew to the depths of his soul.

"I will. . . not. . . do this," he said, and gestured with his fingers to the side, to the side, backward. . . He suddenly turned to Albert.

And it was as though a clear image had appeared on his pallor, before he spoke I already knew for sure that he had not collapsed but continued to direct events, to maneuver them. . . without letting Henia and Karol out of his sight. . . in their direction! So what? Was he afraid? Or was he running after them?

"Not you either," he said straight out to Albert.

"Me?"

"How are you going to do it? . . . with a knife? Because it'll have to be a knife, not a revolver, that's too noisy— how could you with a knife, when your mother was. . . a few days ago with a knife too? You? You, with your mother and your Catholicism? I ask you, how would you do it?"

His words were confused but they were sincere, supported by this face which provoked Albert's face, crying "no!" No doubt—"he knew what he was saying." He knew what was meant by "murder" and was at the end of his tether, could no longer stand it. No, it was no longer a game, or tactics, it was true at this moment!

"Are you deserting?" asked Hippolytus coldly.

In answer he smiled, dazed and disarmed.

Albert gulped as though he were being forced to swallow something inedible. Up till now he must have thought about the problem as I had, on a military level: this murder was just another death, for him, one of many—repellent but usual and even necessary, inevitable. But now it was being extracted from its anonymity and presented to him on its own, like the act of killing himself, immense and terrible! He too turned pale. And his mother, into the bargain! And the knife! The same knife as the one that killed his mother. . . So he would murder with the knife that had just been pulled out of his mother, he would deal the same blow, repeat the same movement on Siemian's body. . . But behind his furrowed brow was his mother not suddenly merging into Henia? At any rate it was Henia, not his mother, who proved decisive. He must have seen himself acting Skuziak's role as he dealt the blow. . . But how would he then behave toward Henia and Karol, how would he resist their union, Henia in Karol's arms, adolescent Henia in his adolescent arms, Henia brazenly "boyified?". . . Murder Siemian as Skuziak had murdered?—but what would he become? Another Skuziak? What would he oppose to this adolescent force? If only Frederick had not magnified and exalted the act of murdering—but now it was the act of himself killing and this knife thrust struck his own dignity, his honor, his virtue, everything with which he defended his mother from Skuziak and Henia from Karol.

That was obviously why he turned to Hippolytus and muttered, as though he were stating a fact:

"Me. . . No, I couldn't do it. . ."

Frederick questioned me, with an almost triumphant look which anticipated the answer:

"And you? Would you murder him?"

Well? What? Was it only tactics? He operated by simulating fear, by forcing us to refuse. Inconceivable: this fear of his, pallid and trembling, drenched in sweat, was nothing but a horse on which he galloped. . . toward those young knees and hands! He put his fear to an erotic use. The height of imposture, a disgrace! Unheard of, intolerable! He treated himself like a horse! But his force took me with it and I felt I must gallop with him. What was more, I naturally did not want to murder. I was happy to be able to get out of it—our collective discipline had already been destroyed. I replied:

"No."

"What a bloody mess," said Hippolytus vulgarly. "All right, that'll do. I'll do it myself. Without any help."

"You?" said Frederick. "You?"

"Me."

"No."

"Why not?"

"Nooo. . ."

"Look," said Hippolytus, "think it over. We can't be pigs. You must have a sense of duty. This is duty! We're obeying orders!"

"Do you want to murder an innocent man out of a sense of duty?"

"It's an order. We've received an order. This is an action. I won't neglect my duty and I hope I can say the same of you. We must do it! We're responsible! What do you want? To let him escape alive?"

"That's impossible," admitted Frederick. "I know. . . "

Hippolytus opened his eyes wide. Had he expected Frederick to reply: "Yes, let him escape alive"? Did he count on it? If that were his secret hope, Frederick's reply had put an end to it.

"Well, what do you want?"

"I know, of course. . . necessity. . . duty. . . orders. . . We can't. . . But you. . . no. . . You can't slaughter him. . . Not you. . . You can't! Nooo. . . "

Hippolytus, confronted by this humble, modest, whispered "nooo," sat down. This "nooo" knew what it was to murder and—all this knowledge turned against him and crushed him. Enclosed in his puffy body he watched us through a sort of window, with bulging eyes. A "straightforward" liquidation of Siemian was now out of the question, after our three refusals. It had turned foul under the pressure of our horror. He could no longer allow himself to be superficial. By nature he was neither profound nor particularly sensitive, but he belonged to a certain social class, a certain elite, and when we became profound he could no longer remain superficial, if only for social reasons. In certain situations it is not permissible to be "less profound" or "less subtle," this disqualifies you socially. So good manners required him to be profound, required him to join us in sounding the meaning of the word "murder," to see, as we had seen, its full horror. Like us he felt powerless. Slaughter someone with his bare hands? No, no, he could not do that. But in this case the only alternative was "not to murder"—"not to murder" was tantamount to betraying, deserting! He spread out his arms, overtaken by the course of events. He was trapped between two nightmares —one of which was to become his.

"What shall we do then?"

"Leave it to Karol."

Karol? So that was what he had been driving at—the fox! The old rake! Spurring himself on like a horse.

"Karol?"

"Of course. He'll do it. You just have to tell him."

He spoke of it as though it were the easiest thing in the world—all difficulty had vanished miraculously. As though Karol were to do some shopping in Ostrowiec. I don't know why, but this sudden change of tone seemed quite justifiable. Hippolytus hesitated.

"Must we leave it to him?"

"Who else? We can't do it, it's not for us. . . But it must be done. You tell him. He'll do it if you tell him. It won't be any problem for him. Why shouldn't he do it? Order him."

"If I order him he'll do it, of course. . . But. . . How shall I put it?. . . He'd be doing. . . our job?"

Albert joined in nervously:

"You don't seem to realize the risk involved. . . It's a responsibility. We can't shift it onto him, make him run this risk, that's impossible. It isn't done."

"We'll take the risk. If it ever comes to light we can say we did it. What's the matter? Take a knife. . . and wham! It'll be easier for him than for any of us."

"But I tell you we have no right to use him. . . Just because he's sixteen. . . we can't put him in this. . . let a child replace us. . . "

He was panic-stricken. Make Karol commit a murder which he, Albert, was incapable of committing, exploit his youth, Karol's, just because he was a child. . . no, it was dishonest, and it weakened him before the boy. . . and he must be strong before the boy! He started pacing up and down the room. "It would be immoral!" he burst out in fury and turned purple, as humiliated as though his innermost thoughts had been revealed. Hippo, on the other hand, was gradually getting used to the idea.

"Maybe, after all. . . Actually, it's the easiest way. . . Nobody's evading responsibility. We're just keeping our hands clean. . . It's no job for us. It's for him."

And he calmed down as though he had been charmed— at last the only natural solution to the problem had been found. He realized it was in accordance with the order of things and calmed down. He did not withdraw. He was there to give orders—Karol to obey them.

He turned to calm and reason. . . He became aristocratic.

"And to think it didn't occur to me! . . . Of course!"

It was a curious spectacle: two men, one ashamed of what had returned dignity to the other. This exploitation of an adolescent filled one with pride and the other with shame, it was as though one of them had suddenly become less masculine and the other more so. But Frederick— what genius! To have brought Karol in. . . to make it all slant toward him. . . thanks to this the intended death suddenly heated up and glowed not only with Karol but with Henia, with their arms and legs—and the future corpse bloomed with all their adolescent, clumsy, rough sensuality. The heat burst inside me: this death was in love. And all this—this death, our fear, our horror, our helplessness—so that this young, this too young hand should be able to seize the girl. . . I already plunged into the event as though it were not a murder but the marvelous adventure of their untried, secret bodies. Exquisite!

And at the same time this decision revealed a cruel irony and something resembling a taste of defeat—because we adults were obliged to resort to this child who was alone capable of accomplishing what was beyond us. Was this murder to be like a cherry on a fragile branch, only accessible to the lightest of us?. . . Lightness! Suddenly everything began to turn in this direction, Frederick, Hippolytus, and I turned toward the adolescent as one turns to a soothing ointment.

Suddenly Albert too came out in favor of Karol. If he had refused he would have had to act on his own because we were already *hors concours*. And then something must have made him change his mind—his Catholicism clearly convinced him that Karol as a murderer would revolt Henia just as much as he, Albert, would as a murderer: an error due to the fact that he sniffed flowers with his spirit instead of using his nose, he believed too firmly in the ugliness of sin and the beauty of virtue. He had forgotten that crime could have a certain taste in Karol's body and a different one in his. And, clinging to this illusion, he agreed to our plan—in fact he had no alternative if he did not want to break away from us and find himself all alone in such a difficult situation.

Frederick, fearing he might change his mind, rushed off to look for Karol; I went with him. He was not in the house. We found Henia hanging up linen in the pantry; but it was not she we wanted. We grew more nervous. Where was Karol? We searched for him feverishly, without saying a word, as though we were strangers.

He was in the stable grooming the horses; we called him and he came up to us, smiling. I well remember that smile because at the moment we called him I realized the folly of our plan. He adored Siemian. He was wholly devoted to him. How could we force him to do such a thing? But his smile immediately transported us to another world where everything was easy and friendly. This child already knew his assets. He knew that if we expected anything from him it was his youth—so he came up to us slightly mockingly, prepared to be amused. And the way he came up to us put us at our ease, it showed how familiar he had become. And

it was strange: this smiling lightness was the best introduction to the brutality that was to follow.

"Siemian's a betrayer," explained Frederick briefly. "It's
been proved."

"Aha!" said Karol.

"He has to be done in today, tonight. Can you do it?"

"Me?"

"Are you scared?"

"No."

He was standing by a shaft with a saddle girth hanging
on it. His fidelity to Siemian did not reveal itself in any
way. When he heard about killing him he became taciturn,
almost ashamed. He shut himself up in his shell. He did
not look as though he were going to protest. I told myself
that for him to kill Siemian or to kill on Siemian's orders
was more or less the same thing—what bound him to
Siemian was death, it did not matter which death. Blindly
obedient and soldierly to Siemian—but obedient and soldierly too when he had to turn against Siemian on our
orders. His blindness toward his leader had turned into the
immediate and silent capacity to kill him. He showed no
surprise.

And yet (the boy) stole a glance at us. There was a
secret in that glance (as though he were asking us: are you
doing this for Siemian. . . or me?). But he said nothing.
He had become discreet.

Slightly stunned by this incredible facility (which seemed
to introduce us to another dimension) we led him to Hippolytus who gave him further instructions: to go there at
night with a knife and above all make no noise. Hippo had
already regained complete self-control and gave orders like
an officer—he was in his place.

"And what if he doesn't open his door? He locks himself
in at night."

"We'll find a way of making him open it."

Karol went off.

That he should go off like that made me wild. Where had he gone? Home? What was his home? What was that world of his where people died as easily as they murdered? In him we had found an obedience and eagerness which proved that he was indeed just the man we needed—it had all gone so smoothly! Oh, he had left so superbly, silent and docile. . . and I could not doubt that it was she, Henia, he had gone to join, with his hands into which we had put a knife. Henia! There was no doubt. Now, as a boy with a knife, a murderer, he was closer than ever to conquering and possessing Henia—and if Hippolytus had not detained us a few moments in the study we would have rushed after him, to spy on him. So it was only some time later that we left the study and made for the garden in search of him, of her. We were already in the hall when we heard Albert's stifled voice break off—something was going on! We retraced our steps. A scene like the ones on the island. Albert two steps away from Henia. . . We had no idea what, but something must have just happened.

Karol was standing further off, by the sideboard.

When he saw us Albert said:

"I've just slapped her."

He went out. Then she said:

"He's pretty tough!"

"He's pretty tough," repeated Karol.

They were laughing. They were mocking. Malicious but amused. Not so much, though—not too much—they were just joking. But with what elegance! And then they enjoyed it, this "he's pretty tough," they looked as though they were reveling in it.

"What got into him?" asked Frederick. "What was he driving at?"

"What do you think?" answered Henia. She turned up her eyes comically, coquettishly, and we immediately realized it was because of Karol. The marvelous part of it was that she did not even have to look at him, knowing that it was useless, that it was enough for her to be coquettish—she knew she could only attract us "with" Karol. How easy it was for us to communicate with them—and I could see they both reckoned on our good will. Cunning, discreetly amused, and fully aware that they enchanted us. That was quite clear.

Evidently Albert must have lost his self-control—they must have wounded him again by an imperceptible glance, a touch. . . ah, these childish provocations! Frederick suddenly asked Henia:

"Has Karol told you anything?"

"What about?"

"That tonight. . . Siemian. . . "

He drew his hand across his throat—a gesture that would have been amusing had the game not had such serious consequences for him. He was having fun in earnest. He sat down. No, she knew nothing, Karol had not mentioned it. He told her briefly what they intended to do that night and that Karol was going to do it. He talked about it as though it were quite unimportant. Both of them (Karol too) listened—they could listen to us because they had to attract us and this slowed down their reactions. Only, when he had finished, she did not say a word—any more than Karol—and we felt the silence rise in them. We did not quite know what they meant. But (the boy) leaning on the sideboard looked sullen and she became sullen too.

Frederick explained: "The only problem is that Siemian might refuse to open the door. He'll be frightened. You could go together. Henia, you could knock for some reason or other. He'll open to you. It wouldn't even occur to him not to open. You could say you've got a letter for him, or something like that. And when he opens you step back and let Karol in. . . I think that's the best plan, don't you?"

He suggested it casually, "like that," and he was right because this plan of attack was pretty dubious; he was by no means sure that Siemian would open his door without any difficulty, and Frederick barely concealed the real meaning of the suggestion, which was to involve Henia. . . to put them in it together. He organized it like a scene on the island. It was not so much the idea that dazzled me as the way in which it was executed: he had suddenly presented the plan, casually, taking advantage of a moment when they were both prepared to be kind to us, to join us, or simply to charm us—both of them! Frederick counted on their "good will," hoping they would easily be persuaded to satisfy him—once again he was reckoning on the "facility," that same facility of which Karol had given proof. He simply wanted them to crush this worm "together". . . From now on the erotic, sensual, amorous sense of the enterprise came into the open—it was quite obvious. For the fraction of a second I thought the two sides of the matter were struggling before us, because on the one hand the proposition was fairly ghastly (were we not plunging this girl too into sin and crime?) but on the other it was "intoxicating and exciting," because they had to perform this act "together."

Which of them would win? I had time to ask myself the question because they did not reply at once. I was well aware, from the way they stood before us, that they always remained reserved, unaffectionate and dry *toward each other*—and yet they were so upset by our amazement, the intoxication we secretly demanded from them, that they were submissive. They could no longer struggle against the beauty we discovered in them. And in fact this submissiveness suited them—were they not made for submission? It was another of these acts committed "on oneself," so characteristic of youth, thanks to which it affirms itself, of these acts the power of which is so intoxicating, that their objective and exterior meaning almost vanishes. For them the most important thing was neither Siemian nor his death—but themselves. The girl just answered:

"Why not? We can do it."

Karol suddenly laughed, rather stupidly:

"If it works we can do it, if it doesn't work we can't."

At that moment I felt this stupidity was necessary for them.

"Very well," he said. "So you knock at the door, and then you slip back and I'll bump him off. It'll work provided he opens the door."

She laughed and said: "Don't worry. If I knock he'll open it."

She too looked rather stupid, just then.

"This is all between ourselves, of course," said Frederick.

"Don't worry!"

Thereupon our conversation ended—conversations of this sort cannot be prolonged indefinitely. I went onto the veranda and then into the garden; I wanted a breath of air —it was hurtling along too fast for my liking. The light was fading. The colors had lost their sheen, the greens and the reds were no longer so dazzling—it was the shady repose of colors before night. What did the night conceal? Ah, yes. . . crushing the worm. . . but the worm was now Siemian, not Albert. . . I was no longer sure whether it was all such a good idea, at moments a dark fire enflamed me, and at others I grew feeble, gloomy, even desperate, because it was all too fantastic, too arbitrary and not real enough— it was always a game, yes, we were "playing with fire."

Wandering into the garden, among the bushes, I lost my train of thought. It was then that I saw Albert striding up to me.

"I want to explain! Please try to see my point! I'd never have slapped her, but she did something revolting—that's all I can say—something revolting!"

"What?"

"She did something revolting. Really revolting, however insignificant. . . no, I know I'm right. . . Something insignificant but really revolting! We were talking in the dining room. He came in—the lover. I felt at once that she was talking to me, but saying everything to him."

"She was saying it to him?"

"Yes, to him. Not in words, of course. . . but with everything. Entirely. She pretended to be talking to me but at the same time she caught him and gave herself up to him. In front of me. Talking to me. Can you believe it? It was quite something. . . I saw she was talking to me and at the same time was with him. . . giving herself up to him! As though I weren't there! I slapped her. And now what can I do? Tell me what I can do?"

"Can't you make it up?"

"But I hit her! I've committed myself. I hit her! Now it's all over and done with. I hit her! I don't know how I managed it. . . You know what? I believe that if I hadn't consented to his being appointed for this. . . liquidation. . . I wouldn't have hit her."

"Why?"

He looked at me sharply.

"Because I'm no longer behaving correctly—toward him. I've let him replace me. I've lost my moral right and that's why I hit her. I hit her because my misery no longer matters. It's no longer respectable. It's been dishonored. That's why I hit her, hit her, hit her. . . and I won't stop at hitting him, I'll kill him!"

"What are you talking about?"

"I'll kill him, and with no difficulty. . . It's of no importance! To kill. . . someone like that? It's like crushing a worm. Less than nothing! But on the other hand to kill someone like that. . . would be scandalous! And disgraceful! It's far harder than killing an adult. It's impossible! Only adults can kill each other. And if I cut her throat. . . Just imagine it! Don't worry. I'm joking. I'm only joking. They're making fun of me. Why shouldn't I make fun of them? Oh God, save me from this joke! Oh God, oh God, you're my only hope! What was I going to say? Oh yes, I'm the only one who has to kill. . . but kill Siemian. . . I should do it while there's still time, I shall have to hurry. . . I can still do it instead of that brat. . . As long as he does it I'm not behaving correctly!"

He pondered.

"It's too late. You've talked me out of it. How can I do this job instead of him, now? If I want to do it so much, it's not out of a sense of duty, but simply so as not to give her to him—not to lose my moral advantage over her. All my morals—just to possess her!"

He stretched out his arms helplessly.

"I don't see what I can do. I don't think there's anything I can do."

He said several more things which left me thinking.

"I'm naked! I feel naked! Oh God! They've undressed me! . . . At my age I should no longer feel naked! Nakedness —it's all right for the young!"

And then:

"She's not only deceiving me. She's deceiving men. Men in general. Because she's not deceiving me with one man. Is she really a woman? Aha, look, she's exploiting the fact

that she isn't a woman yet. They're taking advantage of a
certain particularity of theirs, a certain spe-ci-fi-ci-ty, which
I do not even suspect. . ."

And then:

"I just wonder where they got it from? I've already told
you: they can't have thought it out on their own. The
island. What they're doing to me now. . . This continual
provocation. . . It's too sophisticated. I hope you see what
I mean: they can't have thought it out because it's too
sophisticated. Where did they get it from, then? From
books? How can I tell?"

* * *

Growing blacker and blacker the ink of night leaked out,
confusing everything, and while the crowns of the trees
still bathed in a light, joyful sky of feathers, the trunks
were indistinct and imperceptible. I looked under the brick.
A letter.

You must talk to Siemian.

*Tell him that tonight you will take him out of the house
with Henia and that Karol will be waiting with the horses.
That Henia will knock on his door tonight when everything
is ready. He will believe you. He knows Karol is his and
that Henia is Karol's! He will believe you passionately! It's
the best way to make him open his door when she knocks.*
This is very important. *Please do not forget.*

*And do not forget that we are past the point of no return.
We could only return to disgrace.*

*What about Skuziak? How does he come in? I'm racking
my brains about it. He cannot be left out, all three of them
must do it. . . But how?*

*Take care! We must not force things. Proceed gingerly
and subtly, so as not to arouse anything and not to run any*

unnecessary risks. Until now, thank God, luck is on our side—but we must not spoil it. Look after yourself. Very carefully!

* * *

I went to see Siemian.

I knocked—he opened when he realized it was I, but immediately fell back onto his bed. How long had he been lying there? In his socks—his highly polished riding boots glistened on the ground in a heap of cigarette stubs. He was smoking one cigarette after the other. His long, slender hand with a ring on his finger. He obviously had no desire to talk. He lay on his back and stared at the ceiling. I told him I had come to warn him: he should have no illusions, Hippolytus was not going to let him have any horses.

He made no reply.

"Neither tomorrow nor the next day. What's more, your fear of not leaving this house alive may prove justified."

Silence.

"So I've come to suggest a means of escape."

Silence.

"I want to help you."

He made no reply.

He lay like a log. I thought he was afraid—but it was not fear, it was anger. Rage. He lay there fuming—that was all. Full of venom. That is because (I thought) I have seen into his shame. I knew his weakness, which is why it turned to anger.

I revealed my plan. I told him Henia would knock at his door and that we would take him outside.

"Ff. . ."

"Have you got any money?"

"Yes."

"So much the better. Be prepared—soon after midnight."

"Ff. . . "

"Cursing won't do you any good."

"Ff. . . "

"Don't be too vulgar. We might still change our minds."

"Ff. . . "

I did not go on. He accepted our aid, allowed us to rescue him—but would not say thank you. Lying on his bed, long, muscular, he still expressed force and power— he was the lord and master—but he could no longer use force. It was over. And he knew I knew it. A short time ago he still had no need to beg anyone for help, since he was dangerous and could impose himself by violence, now he lay before me, seething with aggression and rage, but without his claws, compelled to seek compassion. . . and he knew he was unpleasant and unattractive in his emasculated masculinity. . . So he scratched his thigh with his stockinged foot. . . then raised his leg and moved his toes— it was a supremely selfish movement—he did not care whether I liked him or not. . . he did not like me. . . and he was drowning in an ocean of disgust, he wanted to vomit. . . so did I. I went out. This cynicism peculiar to the male sex poisoned me like cigarette smoke. In the dining room I bumped into Hippolytus and I felt sick, I was a hairsbreadth from vomiting, yes, a hairsbreadth, one of those little hairs that grew on our hands! At that moment I could not stand the sight of a man!

There were five of them—men—in the house. Hippolytus, Siemian, Albert, Frederick and I. Ugh. . . Nothing in the animal world attains such deformity—what dog, what horse can compete with this incontinence, with this cynicism of form? Alas! After the age of thirty men lapse into monstrosity. *In their youth the whole beauty of the world was on their side.* I, an adult, could find no refuge with my comrades, the adults, because they repelled me. They pushed me over to the other side.

* * *

Hippolytus' wife stood on the veranda.

"Where have they gone?" she asked. "They've all vanished."

"I don't know. . . I was upstairs."

"And Henia? Haven't you seen Henia?"

"Maybe she's in the orchard?"

She fluttered her fingers. "Don't you feel. . . Albert seems so nervous, so depressed. Has something gone wrong between them? It's as though something had snapped. I'm beginning to worry, I'll have to have a word with Albert. . . or maybe with Henia. . . I don't know. . . Oh God. . . "

She was worried.

"I don't know. But if he's depressed. . . well, after all, he's just lost his mother."

"Do you think it's because of his mother?"

"Of course! We only have one mother."

"Yes. That's what I thought. He's lost his mother, poor thing. Not even Henia will ever replace her for him. We only have one mother! One mother!" Her fingers quivered. And this really calmed her, as though the word "mother" were so powerful that it even removed the meaning from the word "Henia," as though it were the most sacred thing imaginable! . . . A mother! Surely she was one too? Who could claim she was nothing, since she was a mother? This obsolete being who was only a mother and nothing but a mother looked at me with her eyes swimming in perfection and walked away with her cult for the Mother—I knew there was no risk of her getting in our way. Being essentially a mother she could no longer accomplish anything. . .

As she moved away her former charms pranced around her.

*   *   *

As the night crept on with all its heralds—the lighting of the lamps, the closing of the shutters, the laying of the table for dinner—I felt more and more uncomfortable, and I went from one place to another without being able to keep still. Our treason, Frederick's and mine, seemed clearer and clearer: we had betrayed masculinity for (a boy plus a girl). Wandering through the house I glanced into the drawing room, where it was almost dark, and I saw Albert sitting on a sofa. I came in and sat in an armchair some distance from him, against the opposite wall. My plans were fairly vague. Confused. A desperate attempt: to try to overcome my disgust by a supreme effort and come into contact with his maturity. But my disgust increased immeasurably, aroused by my presence here and the position of my body so close to his—increased by his aversion for me. . . an aversion which made me repulsive and made my repulsion for him repulsive too. And vice versa. I knew that in these circumstances it was out of the question for one of us to make use of any of the luxuries available to us—I mean the luxuries of virtue, common sense, devotion, heroism, magnanimity, which we could have manifested and of which we were the potential heirs—but the repulsion was too strong. Could we not overcome it by force? Force? Rape? What were we men for? It is the man who reigns supreme. A man does not ask whether he pleases; he is only concerned with his own pleasure. His pleasure decides what is beautiful and what is ugly—for him, and him alone! Man is for himself alone, not for anyone else!

This was the force I wanted to produce. . . In the present situation both he and I were impotent, since we were not ourselves, we were not for ourselves, we were for that other, younger sensitivity—and this plunged us into ugliness. But if only I could succeed, even for a second, in this drawing room, in existing for him, for Albert, and he for me—if only we could succeed in being a man for a man! How immense our masculinity would be! We would have to force each other to masculinity. This was the calculation on which I based the remnants of a desperate, unconscious hope. Because force, which is the essence of man, must spring from masculinity, from men. . . and maybe my presence alone would suffice to enclose us in this hermetically sealed circle. . . I attached immense importance to the fact that the dark modified our Achilles' heel, the body. I thought that maybe, taking advantage of its enfeeblement, we could succeed in joining each other, affirming each other, that we could become men with enough power no longer to be disgusted by ourselves—because one is never disgusted by oneself, because it is enough to be oneself not to be disgusted! These were my intentions, admittedly already tarnished with despair. But he did not budge, nor did I. . . we could not begin like that, we did not know how to begin. . .

Suddenly Henia slipped into the drawing room.

She did not see me, but went up to Albert and sat next to him in silence. She looked as though she wanted to make everything up. She must have been sweet and gentle (I could hardly see her face). Conciliating. Good. Submissive. Maybe disarmed. Lost. What was happening? Had she had enough of the other one. . . or was she afraid, did she want to withdraw, to find some support or refuge in her fiancé? Anyhow, she sat down sweetly, without a word, leaving the initiative to him. That meant: "I'm at your mercy, do what you like with us." Albert did not budge—not even his little finger.

As motionless as a frog. I wondered what was going on inside him. Pride? Jealousy? Bitterness? Or maybe he just felt guilty and did not know how to behave—and I wanted to shout to him that he should at least embrace her, lay his hands on her, our safety depended on it! Our last chance! On her his hands would regain their sovereignty, I would just have to hop over to them with my hands and it would work! Force—force in this drawing room! But no. Nothing. The time passed. He did not move. And it was like suicide—a failure—a failure—the girl stood up and went out. . . I followed her.

* * *

Dinner was served. Out of regard for our hostess we only spoke about insignificant matters. After dinner I could not think what to do. There would appear to be plenty to do in the few hours before a murder, but nobody looked as though he were doing anything—we all dispersed. . . maybe on account of the excessively intimate and disreputable nature of the plan. Frederick? Where was Frederick? He too had disappeared and this disappearance suddenly blinded me as though my eyes had been bandaged, I no longer knew where I was, I had to find him immediately— so I went to look for him. I went into the garden. It was about to rain, there was a warm moisture in the air, one could feel the clouds gathering in the black starless sky, the wind rose in gusts, weaved through the garden; guessing at the alleys rather than seeing them, treading them with the audacity of unconsciousness, and only the occasional familiar silhouette of a tree or a bush told me all was in order and that I really was where I thought I was. At the same time I realized that I was not expecting this immutability of the garden and that it amazed me. . . I would not have been surprised if the garden had been turned upside down in the dark. This thought made me pitch like a skiff on the high seas, and I realized land was already out of sight. Frederick was not there. I went as far as the islands in a sort of daze and every tree, every bush appearing on my path was an assault of fantasy—because although they were as they were, they *could have been* different. Frederick? Frederick? I needed him urgently. Without him it was all incomplete. Where was he hiding? What was he doing? I came back to the house to look for him again, when I suddenly came upon him in the bushes near the kitchen. He whistled like a street urchin. He did not seem very pleased to see me, and looked almost ashamed.

"What are you doing here?" I asked.

"I'm racking my brains."

"What about?"

"About that."

He pointed to the barred window of the lumber room. At the same time he showed me something in his left hand. The key to the lumber room. "Now we can talk," he said easily, aloud. "Letters are superfluous. She can no longer. . . you know—Nature. . . upset our plans because things have gone too far, the position is too secure. . . We won't have to reckon with her any more! . . . " He said that in a strange way. Something odd emanated from him. Innocence? Holiness? Purity? Anyhow, he was no longer afraid, that was for sure. He tore off a branch and threw it on the ground— before he would have thought twice about it: whether to throw it or not to throw it. . .

"I've brought this key with me," he added, "to force myself to think of a solution to this problem. This problem. This problem of. . . Skuziak."

"Well? Have you thought of one?"

"Yes."

"May I know what?"

"Not yet. . . not now. . . You'll know when the time comes. Or no. I'll tell you now. Look!"

He held out his other hand—in it a knife, a large kitchen knife. "Well, I must say!" I exclaimed, unpleasantly surprised. For the first time I suddenly realized I was dealing with a lunatic.

"I couldn't think of anything better," he said almost apologetically. "But this'll do. *When the young kill the old up there, the old will kill the young down here*—you see? It will close the circle. It will reunite them—him, Henia, and Karol, all three of them. The knife. I've known for a long time that what united them was blood and the knife. Of course it must be simultaneous," he added. "When Karol sticks his knife into Siemian, I'll stick mine into Olek. . . oooh!"

What an idea! A lunatic! A madman! What did he mean—he was going to murder him? And yet on another level this lunacy seemed to be in the order of things and explained itself. This lunatic was right, it could be done, it would reunite them "in a whole". . . . The more bloody and horrible this madness was, the more firmly they would be united. . . And as though this were not enough, this raving thought which stank of the lunatic asylum, degenerate and wild, this nauseating, intellectual idea suddenly gave out the divine, intoxicating scent of a shrub in flower, yes, it was truly sublime! I marveled at it! On another level, on "their" level. This bloody intensification of youth and death, and this union through the knife (of the boy with the girl). It did not actually matter what crime was committed on them—or by them—every cruelty heightened their taste, like a spicy sauce.

The indivisible garden swelled up and gorged itself with charm—although it was damp and misty—around the deformed lunatic. I had to take a deep breath of fresh air, I had just had a bath of marvelous bitterness, of searing seduction. Again everything, everything became young and sensual, even ourselves! And yet. . . no, no, no. I could not agree to it, it was impossible! It had decidedly gone too far! It was out of the question, impossible, this sinister murder of the boy in the lumber room—no, no, no. . . He laughed.

"Don't worry! I just wanted to check whether you still thought I was in my right mind. What an idea! No, not that! It was just a dream. . . from sheer annoyance at not having thought anything up for this Skuziak. It would be monstrous!"

Monstrous. Certainly. When he himself agreed about it the full horror of the plan struck me, as obvious as a plate of roast beef, and I was amazed that I could have been deceived. We went back to the house.

12

There is not much left to tell. In fact everything went very well, better and better, until the finale which, I must admit, exceeded our wildest expectations. And with such ease! . . . I almost had to laugh at the idea of so oppressive a difficulty being solved with such disconcerting facility.

Once again I had to guard Siemian's room. From my bed, lying on my back, I strained my ears—we had entered the night and the house seemed to have fallen asleep. I waited for the stairs to creak under the tread of the two youthful murderers, but it was still too early, there was a good quarter of an hour to go. Silence. Hippo was on guard in the courtyard. Frederick was on the ground floor, by the front door. Finally, at half-past twelve precisely, somewhere below me, the stairs creaked under their feet, which were undoubtedly bare. Bare? Or in socks?

Unforgettable moments! The stairs creaked once more: why were they taking such care?—It would have been far more natural for her to climb the stairs as though there were nothing afoot, and only he would have had to hide, but it was not surprising that the conspiratorial atmosphere had affected them. . . and their nerves must have been on edge. I could almost see them following each other up the stairs, she in front, he behind, groping for the steps with their feet so as to make as little noise as possible. I felt intensely bitter. This furtive approach together was surely nothing but a ridiculous substitute for another approach, a thousand times more desirable, where she would be the object of his furtive steps. . . and yet in this moment their object—not Siemian but his execution—was no less sensual, no less guilty, no less ardent than love, and their furtive approach no less strained. Ah, the stairs creaked again! Youth was approaching! It was infinitely voluptuous, because, under their steps, a horrible act was turning into a triumphant and therefore refreshing act. . . Only. . . only what was this youth that was creeping up, was it pure and really fresh, simple, natural and innocent? No. It was. . . for the adults —if those two were indulging in this venture it was just for us, submissively, to please us, to flirt with us. . . And my maturity "reaching toward" youth had to encounter their youth, "reaching toward maturity," over Siemian's body— this was the appointment.

But there was joy and pride—but what pride?—and something else, like pure alcohol, in the fact that they were conniving with us. At our instigation and also out of a certain necessity to serve us they were running this risk— and creeping up—prepared to commit such a crime! It was divine. It was incredible! It contained the most fascinating beauty in the world! Lying on my bed I literally jumped for joy at the idea that we, Frederick and I, were the inspiration of these legs—ah, the stairs creaked again, but much closer this time, and then nothing, there was silence and I thought that maybe they had given way, that maybe, tempted by this approach together, they had veered from their goal, turned toward each other, and, in a warm embrace had forgotten everything, to depart in discovery of their forbidden bodies! In the dark! On the stairs. Panting. It was not impossible. Was that what had happened? Was it?. . . No, another creak informed me that my hopes were vain, nothing had happened, they went on—and I realized my wish was quite out of the question, absolutely out of the question, not even conceivable, incompatible with their style. Too young. They were too young. Too young for that! They had to reach Siemian and kill him! I thought again (because there was another pause on the stairs) that they had lost heart, she may have pulled his hand to hold him back, they may suddenly have realized the immense weight of their task, its overpowering volume, the horror of the word "murder." Had they discovered that, been stricken with panic? No, never! That was out, too. For the same reason. If that precipice attracted them it was precisely because they could jump over it—their lightness tended toward bloody acts because they could immediately transform them into something else—and their approach to crime was already an annihilation of crime: as they committed it they annihilated it.

A creak. Marvelous, their illegality, this light, furtive (boyish-girlish) sin. . . and I could almost see their legs united in mystery, their half-open lips, I could almost hear them holding their breath. I thought of Frederick, listening to the same furtive noises downstairs, near the front door where he was posted. I thought of Albert, I saw them all, Hippolytus, his wife, and Siemian who must, like me, have been lying on his bed—and I reveled in the exquisite taste of this virginal crime, this youthful sin. . . Tap, tap, tap.

Tap, tap, tap!

A knock. She was knocking at Siemian's door.

It is really here that my story ends. The finale was too. . . smooth and too. . . fast, too. . . light and easy for me to be able to recount it realistically enough. I shall stick to the facts.

I heard Henia: "It's me." The key turned in the lock, the door opened, there followed the noise of a knife thrust and the crash of a body which must have fallen headlong into the corridor. I believe the boy stabbed him two more times as a precaution. I rushed into the corridor. Karol had already switched on his torch. Siemian lay on the floor. When we turned him over we saw some blood.

"That's that," said Karol.

But the face was curiously bandaged by a handkerchief as though he had a toothache. . . It was not Siemian. . . And then, a few seconds later, the truth dawned on us: Albert.

Albert instead of Siemian dead on the ground. But Siemian was dead too—the only difference was that he was on his bed—he lay on his bed, a knife wound in his side, his nose in the pillow.

We turned on the light. I gazed at the scene, filled with a strange doubt. It. . . it did not seem quite true. Too convenient—too easy! I felt vaguely that it could not be like that, like the end of a fairy tale—that Albert had been killed by them and not Siemian! I suddenly realized. This is what happened: immediately after dinner Albert succeeded in getting into Siemian's room through the communicating door between their two rooms. He killed him. Then he waited for Henia and Karol to arrive, and opened the door. He had worked it all out so that they should kill him. To make doubly sure he had switched off the light and wound a handkerchief around his face—so they should not recognize him at once.

The horror of my duality: because the tragic brutality of those bodies, their bloody truth, was the heavy fruit of a supple tree! Those two bodies, those two murderers! As though a fatally definite idea had been pierced right through by lightness.

We went back into the corridor. They looked at him. They said nothing.

We heard someone run up the stairs. Frederick. He stopped, seeing Albert's body. He waved to us—what could he want? He took a knife out of his pocket, held it up in the air for a moment, and threw it on the floor. . . The knife was steeped in blood.

"Olek," he said. "Olek. Here he is."

He was innocent! He was innocent! He exuded innocent naïveté! I looked at our couple. They smiled. As the young always do when they are trying to get out of a scrape. And for a split second, all four of us smiled.